GOOD DUKE
GONE *Hard*
THE GOOD DUKES SERIES

ELIANA PIERS

Please Sign Up

Get my **FREE** Short Story when you sign up to join my mailing list. Plus you'll learn more about me, get sneak peeks at what's in the works, as well as receive access to some discounted or free books from other authors.

Sweeten the Rogue: One wager, one evening of passion, two possible futures for a rogue and a lady

Or use this link here to receive the free ebook: https://bit.ly/SweetenTheRogue

To my Dad,
Thanks for all the chats and plotting sessions
...I should have made him an assassin

Contents

Chapter 1

1815, England

OF ALL THE POSSIBLE reactions Margaret could have imagined she would have upon seeing Jonathan again, she would never have predicted the combination of hugging with all her heart and then slapping with all her strength.

Hugging, yes. Slapping, also yes. But to run up to him, fling herself onto him, hang on for dear life, and then to pull back and slap him for all she was worth? She shook her head at her impulsiveness, for even that behavior surprised herself. Although, truth be told, how can anyone predict their reaction to someone returning from the dead?

With those thoughts racing through her mind, Margaret sat restlessly on her chair as she watched their other houseguest, Mr. Lyle Fairfax, take his oh sweet time to consider his next move on the chessboard. *There were only so many possible moves. Didn't he realize how long he was spending on this one inconsequential move in the grand scheme of life?*

Not that she had callers, luncheons, or balls at the moment. In fact, she was dreadfully, but not irrevocably, bored. Another rainy morning had passed, locking her indoors with her painting. But a woman could only sketch and then paint a bird so many times in so many variations of teal and then chartreuse. Again, a seemingly inconsequential pursuit for someone hoping to be a productive member of society. And although painting was a passion, even that couldn't prevent her restlessness today.

"Dear daughter, that's the third time you've shifted in your seat in the last two minutes," Her Grace, the dowager duchess of Wellingford, Ainsley Campbell chastised. "Please." The single word was half plea half encouragement to sit still or seek out another activity. Mother and daughter being well attuned to each other's moods and communication methods meant small gestures and simple words could convey complex thoughts, even fully plotted schemes, without anyone the wiser.

Margaret raised her eyes to Lyle as he sat leaning forward in his chair with his index finger indenting his chin.

He was lost. Again.

Margaret let out a deliberately long and heavy breath.

No reaction.

She repeated the action, this time adding a vocal hum to the breath.

It was enough to tear his eyes away from the board where she should have been strategizing for her next move. "We can continue this later." He waved her away with a dismissive gesture, far too informal to reflect their roles, but much more representative of the sheer amount of time they'd spent together since Lyle and her brother had gone into business together. Her brother, Gregory, the Duke of Wellingford, had become an investor in Lyle's Vauxhall this past summer. While Gregory was away, Lyle was staying on as their houseguest to offer male camaraderie for Jonathan, along with some moral support.

Indeed, much had happened this summer. But Margaret didn't want to dolefully recall losing her best friend, albeit in marriage to her brother, and being left all alone for the cold, dull winter months. She had no one to blame but herself, since she had just spent the last few months behind the scenes, plotting for Mary and Gregory to finally declare their undying love for each other. Took long enough.

She popped out of her seat. "I'm going out."

Her mother inclined her head and tilted to the gray clouds outside.

"For a short walk."

"Yes, dear," her mother mindlessly answered as she continued her needlework.

What more needlework could their estate need? It had to be going to a charity of some kind.

***

JONATHAN WOODS SAT ON the stone bench overlooking one of the large ponds on the Chatsworth House estates. The pussywillows swayed in the breeze against the flat gray backdrop. It felt like his whole life was flat right now.

Yet the water drew him every day. Sometimes twice a day. And every day, sometimes twice, he answered the call. He had no idea why he came, except that he knew he was searching for and waiting for answers.

Until just recently he had been staying at Glaston Hospital, just off the Bristol Channel, where he knew no one, and no one knew him. More to the point, he remembered absolutely nothing before Glaston. Doctor Phillip Walker became his only reasonable, sane, acquaintance, since Glaston Hospital accommodated the mentally unstable.

He didn't feel unstable. He couldn't feel unbalanced because there was nothing to balance—well, almost nothing.

Dr. Walker had become his friend, so close in fact, that for the last few months, after a near three year stint in the hospital, he stayed with the kind, elderly doctor, helping him around his house and on his calls.

And then one day he woke up and finally remembered something: the name Chatsworth House. Upon telling Dr. Walker, Jonathan was determined to find out what it meant. He had no way of knowing what to expect. Since he wouldn't have been able to sign with his own name–not knowing it–he didn't send a letter first. He just wanted to show up and see it. Impulsive, certainly. Was he impulsive? He didn't know. He could be.

He dropped his head in his hands. He could be anything.

MARGARET HEADED TOWARD THE pond. It was her favorite place to think. If she was feeling warm she could always dip her feet in the water to cool off, and when she was feeling particularly spritely, she just disrobed and dove in for a quick swim.

As she meandered toward the pond, she recalled when she first saw Jonathan back from his disappearance of three long years. She happened to be walking past the front door when fate presented him. He was just standing there in all his golden glory, as if three years hadn't passed, as if her world hadn't turned upside down, deflated, and squeezed of all life.

When she saw him, she stared for a full ten seconds. She knew because she made herself count. Well, she intended to count to ten. She made it to about four when she broke into a run and flung herself at him. All she could think of was that he felt the same, but different. And he smelled...different. But he was the same man. She was touching the familiar nape of his neck, grasping at his hair, pressed against his chest. Her body confirmed that he was indeed the same man that had been her closest friend and heartiest competitor. And so much more. He was the same man, but so, so different.

As she clung to him, she quickly realized his arms hung, unmoving at his sides, so she slid down and looked up into empty eyes. *How could his eyes be so blank after all they had been through? How could he bottle up all of his emotions and hide them within such a hard exterior?* If only she could take that bottle and smash it. She would love to see what he would do then.

But she didn't have a bottle to smash, only a face to smack. And with no response from him, her reaction escalated to compensate. And then after the slap, she ran. She couldn't bear to let him see her so vulnerable while he remained so stoic. She couldn't let him see her holding in all the memories of all the tears she had shed over him.

Only later did she find out he was suffering from something called amnesia. That's what the doctors were calling it anyways. He didn't remember anything. How could he not?

And now he was here, but not. He remembered nothing but the name Chatsworth. Well, what good was that? And, and, and, to top it all off, Gregory, Jonathan's best friend, who would have been the person to help him unlock his memories, was away on his honeymoon. Who knew when they'd be back? Summer. And then everything would change again.

At first Mary and Gregory refused to leave, saying they would help with Jonathan. But Jonathan insisted that they take their honeymoon and spend the winter somewhere warm. He didn't want to be a burden. Gregory had already shared as much as he could with Jonathan, and Jonathan reassured him that he wasn't going anywhere. The doctor that he had been communicating with, recommended that Jonathan stay in one place, undisturbed for a while, in hopes that some memories would come back.

The doctor had no other reasonably helpful advice, just keep him relaxed and around familiar, or what should be familiar, environments. He was not to be upset, jarred, or overstimulated. He was to slowly settle back into whatever memories naturally returned to him.

With Gregory and Mary gone, it all fell to Margaret. Ugh. An impossible task. There were memories she could share, but there were others, precious, that she wanted to keep safe and hers. And far too many memories to sift through all at once.

The pond came into view, and with it, a memory of her and Jonathan.

When she was ten, she had been following Gregory and Jonathan around all morning. At first she tried to be sneaky, but once she knew her efforts were futile, she simply traipsed along behind them, waiting for opportune moments to strike.

Her chance came much later in the day than she had expected, long after any grand schemes she had plotted turned to mush. Standing on the bank, Gregory and Jonathan were arguing over who could swim the fastest when verbal arguing turned physical. At the precise moment that Gregory decided to lash out and shove Jonathan into the pond, Margaret had been directly behind him. So instead of Jonathan splayed out in the pond, Margaret was.

Gregory was bent in half, incapacitated, laughing himself senseless. Jonathan's lips twitched unsure whether to laugh or show concern.

As payback, she decided to take advantage of how little Jonathan knew her. "Help! Help! I can't swim." For effect, she thrashed her arms and kicked her legs. No one was jumping in after her. But she was too far into her prank to let a silly thing like pride, or the need to breathe, pull her out of it. She stopped her thrashing and went belly down in the water, motionless. *One second, two seconds, three seconds...*

And then a huge splash and strong arms were pulling her up out of the water against a lanky but sturdy body. She began flailing her arms again. He deserved it for waiting that long. She didn't care that he was fully clothed and she might be giving him bruises. She was sure they'd be small.

Jonathan bellowed, "Be still!" But then close to her ear, he whispered, "It's on."

She was ten, he was sixteen. It was all innocent fun. The pranks. The challenges. They competed to outdo each other over everything. Fishing, racing, swimming, riding, climbing trees. Of course he always won. Except when he didn't. In those cases he'd always say that he had let her win. She had no way of knowing the truth for certain.

She remembered those days fondly. She would share those memories with Jonathan. Probably. Maybe.

But she would definitely not share all the pond memories with him.

It was nearing the end of summer, right before Jonathan disappeared and right after Margaret had entered society. Margaret was seventeen and Jonathan four and twenty. They were in the middle of an anomalous heat wave.

Margaret had just spent hours tangling herself in sheets, to stay modest, but waking up sweating. Nothing was cooling her down, and she couldn't imagine sitting another second in her damp, dank room. She had woken up just before dawn, so she scrambled to grab a shawl and raced on tip toe out of the house toward the pond. It was calling her. Beckoning her to find relief in its delectable waters.

Down to her nightshift, she slipped into the water. The waters cooled her toes, her thighs, and her thoughts.

Until she heard someone clearing their throat.

"I'm sorry. I didn't know you were coming here." It was Jonathan.

What the hell was he doing here? When did he arrive at Chatsworth? Why can I see his bare chest? And when the devil had his arms grown so large?

Her heart started to race. Mayhap the water was too cold. But then why were her thighs on fire? And why did she feel as though there was a hook in her stomach attached to a line that Jonathan was reeling in to himself?

"I'll leave." She began to pop out of the water, unaware that her nightgown was now entirely translucent.

"Bloody hell," he muttered.

She moved toward him in concern. "Are you alright?"

"Please," he threw his hand over his eyes. "For the love of all that is holy, do not move."

"Why?"

"Just let me think."

"Think–"

"For one second."

"For one second. One!"

"Just–"

"Oh!" Margaret grew alarmed. Something slimy had wrapped itself around her foot. "I'm caught."

"Margaret, please."

"I'm serious, Jonathan. I think my foot is caught in some weeds." He closed his eyes and breathed out slowly, as if he was counting now.

"Listen to me. Do not move. Even one inch." He removed his hand from over his eyes.

"That's impossible. I have to move to stay afloat."

"Just. Don't." He pushed his hands up his face and off his cheeks, in a washing motion. "Please. Let me."

His staccato syntax bewildered Margaret into acquiescence. She tried folding her arms across her chest in defiance, but found her best bet was to swirl her arms, slowly churning the water while she held her legs as still as possible.

As she found her stride of stillness, Jonathan gave her a look. Had she known it was the last look of innocence that would pass between them, she may have tried to memorize it and lock it away into her stash. Instead, she saw some combination of dread, angst, and something else she didn't quite recognize.

Then he ducked his head under the water, and she was never the same again.

Chapter 2

THE SECOND JONATHAN DUCKED under the water, Margaret knew everything had changed. The arm movements to keep herself afloat caused her nightgown to swirl about her waist leaving her bare legs completely exposed to Jonathan. She had no way of knowing whether or not his eyes were open, but it didn't matter. Everything she needed to know she felt in his touch.

Her entire body went on alert as his hand flickered against her hip, then blazed a pathway down her leg to track down exactly where the weeds were. Only, the blaze was not restricted to where his hand touched. Oh, it started there. It sparked there. But it ignited something altogether uncontainable. Her breaths began coming in faster and her arms forgot the pattern they had been mixing to keep her still in the water.

A hand shot up to grab her arms, in all likelihood to keep her still, but the movement shocked her and somehow her free leg had wound itself around Jonathan's back. So at that moment, her left leg was hanging down his back and her right leg was stuck in the weeds in front of him. To her horror, this meant that her honeypot was straddling the top of his shoulder where it met his neck. She was sure that liquid heat was seeping out of her onto his bare flesh. She could feel his ear against her lower abdomen and although she was shocked, and although she should have pushed him away, all she wanted to do was press herself into him more.

And then he went preternaturally still. In hindsight, the moment couldn't have been anything other than the shortest split second pause, yet in that instant a lifetime's worth of thoughts flooded her mind.

This was the man who had always been her fiercest, yet cheeriest competitor. He was one hundred percent reliably the smile she could count on and the jab she could counter. This was the devil may care, all for the love of fun—and the win—man who was her brother's best friend. He was the one who had understood her from the beginning. It felt as though he could read her thoughts, and more frightening, her intentions. He knew just how much to push her in a challenge and how many times he could best her before she needed a win.

And now the heat between her legs was pressing into the side of his neck and the top of his shoulder. She couldn't help herself. Like the force of gravity that pulled Newton's apple down, the same intensity pulled her down onto him.

And then she felt the briefest brush of lips against her inner thigh and her body shattered. Hundreds of thousands of scales fell off her and floated away in the pond. The infinitesimal touch charged through her and the jolt forced her hand into his hair. To what? Hold him there forever underwater? She had no rational thought in the moment, only the undulating sensations caused by his touch.

If only she had predicted his next action, she may have been able to save herself years of heartache, but how was she to know he was just as overwhelmed by arousal and underwhelmed by reason as her? She knew him as carefree, unattached. He had no real emotions. Not really. Until now.

He turned his nose and mouth to the valley between her thighs and nuzzled against her. Her shoulders fell down and her head fell back. All of time stood still and the planet stopped mid-orbit. Where was the sun? It was blazing within her.

If she thought there was a fire before, it had now turned into an inferno. There was no thought, only reaction. She arched into him.

And then waited. Panting.

She felt his forehead against her inner thigh and his hand run down her foot until she felt him pull the weeds away. She was free. In some ways.

She was free to move her leg, but more significantly, she was free to explore this heat and passion.

And then all of a sudden he bobbed out of the water, and they were face to face. She stared into his chestnut eyes. The same eyes that had seen her ride hell for leather ahead of him in their ongoing races. The same eyes that had dared her to look up and always climb just one more branch higher. The same eyes that had seen her as a young girl were now seeing her as a woman, and they weren't looking at her in any way she'd seen before. His eyes had turned dark and they burned into her, like black smoldering embers deceivingly too hot to touch.

She didn't know how, but her legs had wrapped around his waist, with a vice like grip. In a hoarse voice, he whispered, "Are you okay?"

She nodded, having lost all control of her tongue.

"Can you swim?"

She shook her head. Of course she could swim. It's not like a person could simply forget how to swim. But no matter how loudly her mind would have spoken, it couldn't, and her body wouldn't have listened anyways, for it had promptly developed an onset of ankyloglossia.

With one arm lashed around her, he used the other to slowly move them toward the nearest bank. As he began swimming, she panicked.

What would happen now? It was nearly impossible anyone had seen, but that wasn't her concern. She shuddered. Would things go back to normal? Was there a normal that things could return to? What if he were to pretend nothing happened? What if nothing had happened and it was all her imagination? She couldn't quell the barrage of questions in her mind, but she knew that everything felt different, and she also knew that she didn't want it to end yet.

This couldn't be the end. It had hardly begun. How could she live with herself knowing only the foyer to this world of unimaginable and unquenchable heat? And could it be quenched? Could heat be quenched?

These nonsensical thoughts would circle for days if she let them, so instead, she rested her cheek where her honeypot had been moments earlier, and she nuzzled gently into the side of his neck. The corded strength was tempered with the smoothest skin, only to lead into a soft grating nearer to his throat, where day-old stubble must have snuck through his valet's watch.

She thought she detected a stiffening in his body, but she didn't care. He wasn't the only one who could nuzzle. She could nuzzle. She could nuzzle with the best of them. And she would. Whatever that meant.

They reached the bank and he paused before lifting her out of the water and resting her on the grass. Then he pulled himself up beside her, wearing only his smallclothes.

She couldn't stop herself from looking, even if a nabob bought all the elephants from India and stampeded them past her, she would still look at him and take her time. He was chiseled from marble with strong pectorals and a lean abdomen sprinkled with curling gold hairs. His arousal was jutting upward, to push against his drawers. She thought at any moment he would break free. She wished he would.

She couldn't stop herself from touching, even if all her relatives had been present two feet away for an outdoor luncheon. Her fingers followed the trail of golden curls, but stopped just before they led down into his drawers.

She couldn't stop herself from leaning into him, tilting her head up to him, and waiting for his reply.

"Maggie," he groaned.

With more equanimity than she could credit, she replied in a sultry tone, "Johnny."

He looked into her eyes and then let his eyes wander down her body. He paused at her neck, and then her bosom. Just before his eyes ambled down further, she felt his gaze pull her nipples taut. Then his continued gaze stalled on her thighs, stroked down to her toes, and met back up at her eyes again.

No, nothing would ever be the same.

***

JONATHAN TOOK TEA IN the drawing room with a chessboard between him and Lyle. This could be the third or fourth game he was playing, and losing, but he wasn't keeping track. It was merely an activity to keep him occupied for a couple of hours a day to stimulate light mental activity. Lyle was good enough company, though he had refrained from disclosing anything personal and remained something of a mystery. But who was he to judge someone on being a mystery? He had shared nothing either. After all, he had nothing to share

He had found out some news via Gregory that should have elicited a swell of emotions from him. Apparently he had been betrothed, and his fiancee had given up on waiting for him and found a new husband within a year of Jonathan going missing. His mother and father had passed away when he was a boy, and his older brother had passed away while Jonathan was at war, thus making Jonathan the rightful Duke of Somersby. Some paperwork needed to be resolved, now that he had shown up, but Gregory promised to handle that upon returning from his honeymoon. Gregory had only filled in a few gaps about the actual disappearance, telling Jonathan that he had joined the army and after a few months had gone missing. His disappearance had remained a conundrum despite all the inquiries Gregory had made over the years. The War Office disclosed nothing other than approximate dates and times Jonathan had gone missing.

Jonathan should have felt disturbed, desolate, even relieved for at least knowing something of his identity, but no emotions surfaced. Only numbness reigned. And a slight irritation at having no other emotions to manage. His heart was as hard as granite, waiting for something, anything to blast through and thus enable him to be himself again.

As Jonathan waited for Lyle to make his next move, he thought back to the baffling slap, wishing it had at least triggered a crack, or shaken some stones loose.

Fortunately for Jonathan's pride, no one had witnessed it. Or unfortunately, as he had no one to verify or explain its occurrence. Since Dr. Walker had reiterated the need to be in a calm and familiar environment, he didn't want to stir up any drama by involving anyone into his affair. And he wasn't sure he wanted to discuss anything with Margaret yet, especially since he didn't know her and wasn't sure how to address it. Sure, he could just go up to her and ask her, but what if she denied it? Or denied answering him? What if she explained it and was unjustified? Worse, what if her explanation was justified? None of the aforementioned scenarios landed him an answer he liked, so for now he chose the path of least dramatics and pondered it for himself.

But when he wasn't scrutinizing the slap, he was most certainly contemplating the embrace before it. He knew the moment she noticed him because her eyes transformed. The fire that illuminated her eyes took his breath away. Uncertain as to the significance of the fire, he was unprepared for her full body flinging on to him. For that he was most sorry because he couldn't remember if he put his arms around her, though if he had he was sure he would remember the size and shape of her trim waist in his heavy hands. Yes, for that delayed reaction and therefore inaction, he was most sorry.

Now he might never have a tactile memory impressed into his hands.

But mayhap that was best. This was not the time for him to be thinking about taking a lover, or a wife. And Margaret was definitely wife material. But no, her flowing flaxen locks and perfectly proportioned curves were off limits. He had abstained from taking a lover for the last three years, and he could continue. He could not give himself to someone right now, not knowing exactly who he was giving.

Besides, he was a guest here, and he was choosing the path of the least dramatics. Intimacy leads to drama. Ergo, no intimacy, no drama. The perfect plan. It was foolproof.

Jonathan leaned back in his chair wondering if Lyle had made his move yet. He stared at the board but all he perceived were ebony and ivory pieces randomly positioned on a checkered ebony and ivory board. Nothing had changed.

"Must be hard," Lyle said.

"What's that?"

"Thinking of your next move against such a Corinthian at chess."

"I must say I'm a bit surprised to find you're not just a tulip." Lyle's chuckle burst the melancholy hovering over Jonathan.

"Nor a whippersnapper." He jumped off his chair, ducked his head protecting it with his right and twisting to the side.

"A southpaw?"

"Quick observation. I see you haven't lost all memories and knowledge. Glad to know you're no mindless wooden spoon. I wasn't sure based on your chess game,"

Jonathan popped up and mirrored Lyle's posture, light on his feet. "At least you're not bilking me for all I'm worth. We both know you could." Smiling, his body decided it felt right to engage in the playfight. He touched his left foot forward and feigned a jab then crossed right. Lyle ducked and swatted the hand away.

Then Lyle feinted left and crossed right. Jonathan tapped it away and then stood back surveying his opponent.

"I can't remember why I know how to do that." Jonathan mused.

Lyle exhaled and repeated his earlier phrase. "It must be hard."

Jonathan raised a brow.

"Not knowing."

Jonathan waited for him to continue. He didn't know if Lyle was going to spring him or spar him. Unexplainably, Lyle punched him in the gut in a different fashion.

"But you know, you're a man. All men know how to fight...ish. Just...be who you want to be now. Don't worry about who you were. The you of the past made mistakes. Maybe you'll never know them. Maybe you will know them again, but then you'll never be able to forget them. What's worse?"

Jonathan shrugged, unsure of how to navigate deep waters with the nigh stranger before him.

Unperturbed, Lyle continued. "It doesn't matter what's worse. All you have is what is. And right now you don't know who you were. Too bad. Move on. For now. If things change, then deal with that then."

Jonathan nodded slowly, accepting the simple message from the offhand philosopher. "That may be the best advice I've received so far."

"Can't be. The best advice you'll ever receive is to not forget to go for the body." With that he ducked and feigned two jabs to Jonathan's left kidney, then bobbed back up and slapped him on the shoulder.

Lyle pointed at the chessboard, "Shall we call it a day?" he ventured.

"That's a fine plan. I seem to have lost the strategy."

"All good ol' chap." Lyle thumped him on the back. "You'll pick it up on your turn tomorrow."

Lyle turned to head out the door and passed a footman delivering a letter to Jonathan. He paused to pick some imaginary flint off of his waistcoat and then adjusted his cuffs while watching Jonathan's reaction to seeing the name on the letter. When he discreetly observed Jonathan's demeanor unchanged, he inquired, "Tomorrow then?"

Jonathan confirmed, "See you tomorrow." Then out of character, or perhaps within his forgotten character, he added, "Bring your best game though. I've no time for gibfaced foozlers."

Lyle barked a laugh as he made his egress.

Chapter 3

T HE NEXT MORNING, AFTER painting hadn't helped to calm her, Margaret made her way down to the stables to ride away some of her energy. She didn't want to be a bucket of nerves for the upcoming house party her mother was hosting.

As Margaret closed the distance to the stables, she could hear the horses whinnying and imagined herself galloping across the fields, leaving behind unanswered questions and unmade decisions.

But those pesky questions and decisions would plague her until the breeze could whip them away.

She had been avoiding being alone with Jonathan, not really knowing who he was, what to expect, or what to say. She couldn't decide which memories to share with him and which to let go, and the indecision was creating a hollow void in her heart. Was she being more fair to herself if she shared or hid memories? Was she being fair to Jonathan?

The buren she carried weighed heavily. She knew it was up to her to help Jonathan, despite no one explicitly having said so. It would do him good to tour the estates, be reminded of–some–past activities, and see the part of his memory that had finally flashed back to him, so the doctor had suggested in letters that Jonathan had shared with them.

But still she had avoided him. Indecision, however, was not her *modus operandi*. Like, when she was hungry. She wasn't one of those women who couldn't decide what to eat. She had a tried and true method for knowing exactly when she wanted chicken or beef. And she hadn't been in the mood for sausages lately.

In fact, that was the reason she was still single at two-and-twenty. It wasn't for want of offers. She had refused them all, every season since she was eighteen. She was waiting for the perfect love match, and she knew she would know it when she felt it. Or so she thought.

Love was the only good reason to marry, according to Margaret. Her mother had been patient the first few seasons, but now expected that Margaret marry by the end of next season. It was up to Margaret to accept an offer. She knew she would receive offers. It wasn't even arrogant to think it. She was the sister of a duke with a hefty dowry, and–according to more than one poet–possessed the likeness of an angel.

To hell with angels, she wanted to be known for her competence. She didn't mind a challenge, in fact, she thrived on them. Why was it that all men wanted to see was what they could see? Didn't anyone want to look deeper?

Attend to your hair. Check your posture. Back straight. Head still. Don't laugh too loud. Don't smile too big.

And though it was never explicitly said, *never, ever be better than your husband.* With that mandate, Margaret interpreted it to mean she had to find a very competent husband.

Margaret watched Henry pull out the saddle for Wildfire, her sorrel.

"Looks like a good day to ride. Not too cold, not too hot." Henry idly chatted.

"Yes, we are having fine weather."

"Perfect weather for riding. Seems like everyone is in need of the exercise today."

"Oh?"

"Ya, both of your houseguests came here this morning. First Mr Fairfax and then the duke. He was just here. Too bad you missed His Grace just a few minutes ago. Not sure he knew where he was riding to this morning. Seemed as though he might have got himself lost with how long his ride was."

"Oh? He was just here then. I hope he enjoyed his ride." Margaret attempted nonchalance. Not her strong suit, "What was he planning to do after his ride?"

"Oh this and that." She couldn't be sure, but she thought Henry was toying with her.

"Any specific category of 'this' or 'that' mentioned?"

He winked. "Now that you mention categories, he did say that he was going to do some shooting practice. Not sure if he remembers how to shoot a gun." He chuckled to himself. "Hope he doesn't blow his foot off, he's got enough on his mind." He scratched his head, and mumbled, "Or maybe not enough."

Forgetting decorum, she lightly whacked her thigh with the palm of her hand, "Forget the saddle, Henry. I'm going shooting."

What better way to face the man than with pistols present? Guns blazing and all.

JONATHAN STOOD SILENTLY EYEING the target twenty paces in front of him. There was not a sound. Even the birds were quiet. There was no movement in the trees or the clouds. It was fitting that the sky was a dismal gray blanket and the air was stale.

He eyed the pistol in his hand and ran his thumb over the polished wooden handle and brass plating. How did he know it was a double barrel flintlock? Why did it feel natural in his hands? *Must be the army,* he told himself.

He had decided to take Lyle's advice, so for the morning he went for a ride and was now channeling his energy into shooting practice, the first of his working memory. Yet, it didn't feel like the first.

He remembered Glaston fondly, or mostly. Of course, there were headaches, pain, dizziness, and slow progress in the beginning. It was all enough to deter him from putting any efforts into investigating himself. And then he had started to build a bit of a life with Dr. Walker, and it didn't feel pressing to search.

"You still a crack shot?" The question came with a breeze, dispersing his clouded thoughts. Clad in a crimson riding habit, with blonde wisps prancing against her neck, Jonathan held his breath. Light. Energy. Movement. It all emanated from her without effort. Yet, he could somehow inexplicably feel that she was holding something back. Despite that, she brought with her the full force of life and energy, stirring every cell in his body. To do what, he didn't want to know. But she was Aphrodite and Athena rolled into one.

"I'm not sure." His gaze stole back down to the pistol in hand. "I don't actually remember ever shooting one of these."

Margaret took a step back, hands up. Jonathan laughed softly, "Although I don't think you have any cause for concern, I can make no promises." He stood tall, and then tilted his head, "Are you still... a crack shot? Or whatever you were?"

Margaret grinned. If before she emanated light, energy, and movement, now she released the stars. He felt like he knew that glittering smile, that somewhere in the recesses of his mind, he had seen it before. But of course he had. They had all been friends, so he's been told. He had probably seen it a million times. It meant nothing.

"I'm just hopeful each shot can hit the target at all," she said.

Knowing nothing about the woman in front of him, he could still read that she was playing coy. He wasn't sure what game she was playing or why, but he knew the game. "Of that, I doubt."

Her eyes questioned him.

"I doubt you're particularly *hopeful* of anything. I'm sure you simply *know*. And I'm also sure you'll hit dead center."

She began a steady pace toward him. He froze. Even though he had already predicted that she couldn't walk away from a challenge. The closer she got to him, the more his body buzzed with her energy, and when her fingers grazed his as she took the pistol from his hand, he felt lightning shoot up his arm.

What was it about this woman? Was she the reason he had found himself remembering the name Chatsworth?

BANG! He didn't have time to ponder any further.

"Looks like you were wrong."

He surveyed the target, seeing that the hole had just barely found the haystack.

"How do I know you didn't do that on purpose?"

She shrugged. "Shall we put forth a wager?"

"I'm a gentleman. I don't place bets with ladies."

MARGARET'S EYES NARROWED. She wished her eyes were pistols and she could prove her abilities aiming at an apple on his head this very moment.

Was he not going to compete with her based on her gender? He didn't place bets with ladies, did he? How many wagers had he placed and won over the years? Collecting every bloody time. This was assuredly not the same Jonathan.

She pushed aside the niggling thought that he had instantaneously called her earlier bluff the way no one else seemed to be able to do.

Jonathan extended his arm, palm up. She placed the gun in his hand, being sure not to touch him this time. Last time the jolt running through her had almost made her lose her balance. Perhaps that's why her shot went so wide.

BANG! She looked up at a perfect shot.

"Give me that." She wasn't sure if she heard a low chuckle, but she wouldn't have paid any heed to it anyways.

BANG! "Damn." Wide again.

She stopped to reload. BANG! "Bloody hell," she muttered, and this time she was sure of the chuckle.

"What the blazes is so funny?" she demanded.

He straightened his face looking a tad shocked. Maybe that was too harsh. But it wasn't too harsh. This was Jonathan. She could just be whoever she was or wanted to be in the moment and he had always accepted her. Where the hell had that Jonathan gone, and who the devil was here now?

She knew she had to soften her approach. That's what ladies did. She should have more control over her demeanor and not allow others to rile her up. But she didn't dare utter an apology. In fact, she hardened her gaze and repeated, "Well?"

Jonathan hardened his gaze right back. "Well," he took two paces toward her, decreasing the space between them to a handful of inches. "For starters, you need to make a few tweaks."

"Tweaks?" She didn't mean to squeak the word, but he was so close she could feel his warm breath on her cheeks.

And then he placed his hand on her lower back, turning her square to the target. She commanded her body to remain solid and upright while her legs threatened to mutiny her. She didn't remember the other adjustments he made, only that with each touch she instructed her body to stay still. *Do not turn toward him. Do not lean into him. Do not. Do not. Do not.*

He took a step back and cleared his throat. "Yes, that looks better." He motioned toward the target. "Go ahead."

BANG! Still wide.

"Hmmm..." As he eyed her up and down, she shivered. And then prayed to God that he didn't see that. That perhaps God took mercy and temporarily blinded him for the fraction of a second the shiver took to run up and down her spine. Or more realistically the sun blinded him. Yes, the sun. She resolved that the sun was in fact in cahoots with her.

"Upon closer inspection...I see something I missed." He tapped his finger against his chin. "The raised gooseflesh. You're cold."

Damn you, sun.

He shrugged out of his jacket and stepped behind her to help her slip into it. The intimacy of the moment nearly shattered her. The warmth of the jacket seeped into her skin, and, in spite of her best intentions, her soul. She wanted to lift her shoulder to her ears and pull the jacket tightly around her. She wanted to back into him and let his arms wrap around her as they once had.

But she couldn't. He didn't remember. And she wasn't even sure she wanted him to.

So instead of wallowing, she raised her arm and took aim.

BANG! Dead center.

***

THAT NIGHT JONATHAN NEEDED to take his mind off of the enticing woman he'd spent his afternoon with, so he sat in his guest bedchamber rereading a letter from Dr. Walker.

Dear Jonathan,

Or should I say, Your Grace, now? I can't say I'm surprised. There has always been a steady, unassailable confidence in you.

I'm delighted to hear that you have learned more in regards to your identity. I believe you made the right choice in venturing to Chatsworth. Rest assured, more information will trickle in. Be patient.

Take each day, moment to moment. You never know when you might wake up.

Ironic, that. Considering Jonathan couldn't even get to sleep this particular night. All he could think about was Margaret when what he should do was exert his energy uncovering his true identity. How had he ended up in Glaston hospital? Who was he before Glaston? Why had the name *Chatsworth* finally emerged from cloaked memories?

Jonathan sent a reply to Dr. Walker kindly thanking him for his support and inviting him to visit at Chatsworth and join the impending house party, if he was able.

It was a touch lonely at Chatsworth, so he welcomed a familiary face. It was unfortunate that Gregory had left on his honeymoon so shortly after Jonathan arrived on his doorstep, but he couldn't expect the man to delay his life for him. He didn't want to be a burden.

Truthfully, he had to be grateful for Lyle, the dowager duchess, and Margaret. Lyle was good company, but he couldn't spend all day following the man around. Besides, Lyle also had his business to run, the pleasure gardens of Vauxhall. The dowager duchess was kind and patient, albeit preoccupied with planning every last detail for the house party. So that left Margaret.

Perhaps fate had aligned these events in perfect tandem to force him to rely solely on her as the linchpin holding his memories together.

Yes, she was the linchpin. He would collect every memory he could from her. He knew she was holding something back and—dammit—if they were his memories, he had a right to them.

Forget her champagne colored tresses and deep chocolate eyes. Forget her pert breasts jutting out as she shot the bullseye draped in his jacket. Forget how his jacket now lingered of her faint jasmine scent. Forget her as a woman, and think of her as the holder of his memories.

Forget that he had taken all leave of his senses during their shooting practice when he had instinctively touched her, moved her body at his whim, and had then imagined arranging her arms and legs in a few other positions. No, overstepping in the shooting practice was for the exclusive purpose of coaching her to take a better shot. And she had done.

With that resolved, all Jonathan could think about was the burning imprint left on his hand from earlier. With certainty now, he knew that he knew that waist.

Chapter 4

T O HELL WITH HIM and his warm sandalwood scented jacket. She didn't need his help fixing her aim, and she sure as hell
didn't need him in her life.

If he stayed as he was, there was no point in behaving as if they had
a history, since he didn't remember it. And if he recalled everything,
she was disinclined to clear the air between them anyways. It had been
too long. She had moved on. And so she would keep moving on.

It was decided. She wouldn't tell him anything more than what
he absolutely needed to know, which, in her opinion, was next to
nothing.

Sure, he might remember everything, but the devil she would help
restore memories that would only lead to an affray between them.

Yes. This was the healthiest choice to lead her into next season when
she would choose a husband for herself. With someone who hadn't

torn her heart to shreds. With someone who would respect her mind and then worship her body. Preferably in that order.

No. There was no way she wanted to revisit their last moment together. He walked away unscathed. She was the one left with an ache so great, and so forbidden, she could do nothing but pretend it never existed. His disappearance was the best thing that had ever happened to her. It facilitated the pretense seamlessly.

That's what she told herself. And that's what she kept telling herself with each step she took toward the breakfast room.

JONATHAN SENSED MARGARET ENTER the breakfast room before he heard or saw anything. Her energy and presence swept into the room like whispering clouds and blue skies. When his eyes scanned her figure, a tight throb began in his groin. From yesterday's shooting practice, he could feel his hand on the small of her back slipping around to her waist and down her hip. He caught her breasts bobbing with every breath, neatly tucked into her rose colored day dress.

She was the keeper of his secrets. He knew it now. He felt it everywhere. And he would use every charm in his arsenal to uncover those secrets. He didn't care what rake he would have to channel, nor did he care how many layers he had to peel back. Oh yes, he would peel back all the necessary layers.

"Good morning, Margaret. Nice of you to join us today," Lyle looked up from spooning jam onto his bread. "It is quite fortuitous indeed, since today I have to abandon Jonathan and leave him without a chess partner this morning. Since you're here, you can take my place."

Jonathan muffled his groan with a cough. He had been more than content to be relieved of a chess game this morning. Not that he didn't appreciate Lyle's male company, the lord knew he needed it.

But then again, mayhap this was his chance to start the game with Margaret.

He watched Margaret load her plate with pound cake, toast and various preserves from the sideboard.

"Lyle was just telling me that he had some business to attend to in town today."

Margaret turned to Lyle and smiled, "I hope you have a pleasant journey."

"Thank you. I should be back this evening. It's only a few decisions to make on some new features to be placed in the gardens. Apparently it can't be done via mail." He shrugged one shoulder.

"I'm sure it'll be nice to have a change of scenery," Margaret flicked her gaze at Jonathan.

"As someone who has had more than their fair share of changes in scenery, I must laud the familiar."

He thought he heard a tiny feminine harrumph, but he wasn't sure. What he did hear with certainty, was Lyle's chair sliding back. "Both excellent points to consider as I ride to London and back today." He tipped his head and made for the door.

"Well, I for one, cannot wait for our first chess match to begin," he paused. "This will be our first time, won't it?"

He saw her knuckles clench around her knife.

"It doesn't matter, does it?" She asked.

"I should like to know who has the advantage."

"You don't seem to believe me when I do tell."

"Perhaps I wouldn't. That's for me to decide."

Raising steadily from her chair, Margaret squared her body to his. "Is it always for you to decide?"

"It is." His eyes fixated on her.

"When is it not?"

"It always is. Though it may not be for me to decide the thoughts that seep into my mind, it is always for me to decide which thoughts reside there. And it is always for me to decide what to say and how to act, based on those thoughts."

"Exactly." She placed both palms down on the table and leaned forward. Her eyes had darkened to autumn storm clouds, but her parted lips looked like a deep well, a perfect place to dip in for a drink.

He shook off the imagery forming in his mind, stood up, and mirrored her pose until they were nose to nose.

"Drawing room. Twenty minutes."

"Fifteen." She countered.

***

FIFTEEN MINUTES? MARGARET QUESTIONED her sanity. There was no rational explanation for why she had to counter the offer of twenty minutes, except...him. Oh, how he got under her skin. She had to rise to the challenge and beat him.

So with three minutes to spare, she was in the drawing room tapping her toe when he entered. "You're late." She didn't turn to look at him.

"I believe I have two minutes."

"Early can still be late."

He cocked his head at her and walked over to the chessboard.

She held out two downward facing fists to him.

"What's this? First shooting, now boxing? I may not have needed to teach you much in shooting, but I can clearly see you require more than a little guidance in boxing."

"Pick one."

"Left."

She opened her fist revealing a white pawn for him to take, but rather than let him take it from her palm, she placed it on A2. Then she began setting up the black pieces for herself.

The silence continued until after they had each made their first moves.

"Who usually wins between you and Lyle?" His baritone trickled through her.

She eyed him and repeated her earlier question, "Does it matter?"

"I'm having deja vu. Can amnesics have that?"

She stifled a smile. He always knew how to provoke her, into a grin or into a fury. That's why he had been so dangerous. And divine. She never had to hold back laughing with him, nevermind concern herself with showing her teeth in a smile. She never had to hold back her barbs either. She never had to hold back herself from him. He had accepted it all. Encouraged it all.

But now, she would not give him the satisfaction of her joy. He didn't deserve it. "I'm sure they can. Even you have, what, three years of memories now?"

Ignoring her probe, he circled back to his previous topic. "I shouldn't be saying this, or maybe you would have already guessed it, but Lyle always comes out on top. I rather think he's staying on as a houseguest just to boost his ego."

The corner of her mouth creeped to the side, but she ordered it back. In an effort to bore him to death, she posed as if considering her next move. As she did so, he leaned back and pushed his hessian boots forward, almost touching her slippers under the table.

She pulled her feet back, she couldn't be close to this man in any way. The last time that had happened, they had enjoyed a few glorious weeks together. Then one night it all ended and she thought she'd never see him again.

Their last night... It was one in the morning, and Margaret heard a familiar pattern tapped out on her door. Clad in her chemise, she slowly opened the door, hiding behind it.

Jonathan whooshed in on a breeze, closing the door behind them, and caging her in between his arms and the door. Pressed against the door, with him sentinel, she was safe. The gooseflesh raised on her skin, signaling the pleasure to come, and she knew he would do nothing to harm her.

"I couldn't wait," he whispered in her ear.

She threw her arms around his neck. "Wait until when?"

"Until any time past now. I had to see you."

Her heart rocked against her chest and she leaned into him, wishing there were no layers between them. Even one light chemise was one too many.

"See?" As his lips trailed down her neck, she couldn't make out any more words than the echo of his.

"See. Kiss. Lick." He slowly grazed his teeth down the column of her neck and nipped down slowly at the bottom.

A moan escaped her as she pressed herself into him. His long, thick arousal pressed tight against her belly.

"Mmm...Johnny."

"Maggie." He poured his liquid honey voice all over her body. She could still hear him saying her name. She could still hear him, actually, right now, in the drawing room.

"Margaret?" Jonathan's voice pulled her back to the present, and she could feel herself blushing. That's when she noticed her slippered feet had slid back to where she had earlier retreated from. They were now cradled by his boots. Hence the warmth pooling between her thighs. *Had he noticed? How could he not?*

Mortified, but with no other course of action, she reacted by pulling her feet away and hopping out of her seat, "I had just played out the next eight moves in my head when you had to go and interrupt me." She waved her arms accusingly at him. "Can you comprehend that I'm silently strategizing?" In her rant, she had lost count of her physical movements and now thought she only had one move left. She turned her back on him.

Facing the window, she regained her composure. Then she turned and sat down, smoothed her dress, and resumed her concentration on the chess board as if nothing had happened.

JONATHAN TOOK INVENTORY OF the woman in front of him. As sure as he knew he was sane, despite a somewhat debilitating mental condition, he knew the woman in front of him was not. Most assuredly she was bat crazy.

First, she slipped her feet between his, in some attempted flirtation. Then she turned around acting as if he were the one who violated some unspoken rule regarding talking during a chess game. Finally, she pretended as if nothing happened. Yes, she was definitely crazy.

But, he had also seen how all of this was a cover up for how she had been affected by the touch of their shoes. Maybe extracting his secrets was going to be easier than he thought. Maybe channeling the rake was his next move.

He sat back in the cushioned armchair and ran his hands slowly over the polished wood. He turned to look out the large window overlooking the perfectly manicured gardens behind the house. His eyes observed the forest green drapes secured with gold cords, but his mind recalled Margaret's reflection in the window from moments ago. He saw her deep blush and the way she collected herself. Yes, he knew without a doubt that he could have an effect on her. To what extent? With what success? He wasn't certain. But he could feel a familiar sensation within his mind, as if returning some essence of him without the memories.

The rest of the game was played in relative quietude with only the click and sliding of pieces. Both players silently determining their next moves on and off the board.

Until,

"Check."

"Forty-eight."

"Check."

"Forty-nine."

"Check"

"Fifty. Stalemate."

Chapter 5

MARGARET SAT ON THE magenta settee against the cream and gold gilded walls in the parlor. Her mother, the dowager duchess, had been working steadily on her needlework all morning while Margaret flipped pages in her book without taking in any words.

"Have you avoided him long enough now?" Her mother didn't need to explain who *he* was.

"I'm not avoiding him. In fact, we just practiced shooting the other day. And played chess yesterday." Margaret closed her eyes and nodded her head once.

Her mother continued to prick the needle through the fabric, working on a ruby red rose. "So have you ceased your eschewance then?"

Margaret rolled her eyes with her lids pulled down.

"I can still see that," her mother said, still picking at the rose.

Margaret sighed. She hadn't told her mother everything that had happened between her and Jonathan, but if anyone suspected something the summer she had turned eighteen, it would be her mother. She would be mortified if her mother knew the full extent of what happened. She would be ruined. There would absolutely, and terrifyingly so, be a scandal. Gregory would have to pull in favors to prevent it from spreading, if that were even possible. He would probably also have to increase her dowry. Then, she would likely be chaperoned wherever she went doing whatever she did, compared to the unconventional freedom she currently had. And this was understating it. Likely she would end up marrying the first willing man Gregory could find for her. Oh, it would be awful if anyone found out about how Jonathan had entangled himself with her.

"What are you suggesting, mother?" She knew exactly what her mother was suggesting.

"He's just a man, dear."

Just a man. What were those words supposed to mean? He was not just a man. He was, or had been *her* man. And then he had become the missing man. And now he was the man who had returned from the dead, like Lazarus. She could now relate to Mary and Martha, except not at all because she had no soreital feelings for him. God, how she wished he was just a man. Knowing what she had to do would be so much simpler if he was just a man.

Margaret didn't want to tread water in these thoughts any longer, "I'm going out."

"Yes, dear." With such focus, her mother's current needlepoint project would brandish the most intricately threaded rendition of a ruby red rose the world had ever seen.

On her way out the door, Margaret flagged down Bugsby, the beanpole of a butler, and asked him of Jonathan's whereabouts.

"I believe he is in the library, my lady. Shall I ring for him?"

"No, I'll go find him myself."

He bowed as she marched off. When she arrived at the library door, she didn't hesitate to waltz in, swinging the door with perhaps more force than necessary.

It was a library, so of course it would make sense for Jonathan to be found reading a book. What Margaret didn't expect was to find him without his cravat or jacket, poring over Debrett's.

In his past life, Jonathan would have volunteered for a boxing match, a duel, perhaps even cleaning the stables, before willingly opening and studying the book of etiquette and social class.

Margaret felt a catch in her breath against her ribs and a heaviness sit there. *I hear you, Fate, but damn you.*

She had to coral her emotions, the ones given to pity, but more so the ones starting to heat up between her thighs as she longed to lean forward for a clearer view of the golden curls twisting at his collar.

She pointed to the book, "The weather hasn't been that bad for that long, has it?" The weather. Always a safe opening.

Jonathan looked up and rubbed his thumb knuckles across his eyelids. When his once smooth, now calloused hands from the war had finished massaging life back into his eyes, she noticed the shadows pulling down on his face.

"Looking anywhere for clues and triggers."

Margaret inclined her head.

"Dr. Walker encouraged me to pursue any and all possibly familiar trails as they could be the key to unlocking my memories. Or as he puts it, I never know when I might wake up."

"Wake up? Does it feel like a dream then?"

"Sometimes."

"And others?"

He paused. She knew she was pushing him. Why was she pushing him? Did she want to punch him in the gut just to see if he still felt pain? But she couldn't help her curiosity.

"Other times it feels more nightmarish."

Margaret ignored all of her wildly exploding impulses to reach out to him physically and ease his emotional pain. When ignorance failed, like a sergeant, she commanded her arms to hang casually at her sides, her feet to remain planted in their current footprints, and her torso not to sway forward deceitfully forcing her feet and arms to follow.

With nonchalance foreign to her, she asked, "Which familiar trails have you ambled down?"

"That's the problem. Nothing is familiar." He threw up his hands and exhaled. "I know things are supposed to be familiar. But they aren't. So I thought, mayhap if I started at the root, or the tree I suppose, my family, something might be triggered. Even if I just find one trail, it could be the answer." He pushed his hands into and up his cheeks, and then leaned back in his chair.

"Let's go then."

JONATHAN WATCHED AS MARGARET swiveled on her heel and strolled out of the room. He could have said no. Or no thank you. He could have asked why. He could have even ignored the entire scene, saying nothing. He could have sat all morning, or at least a few more minutes, studying Debrett's.

Instead, he snatched his coat and followed her sashaying hips draped in a murderously tight aquamarine morning dress out the door.

"To the theater," he heard her call.

As they entered the opulent room, he noticed the garnet red drapes flowing across what looked like a pristine wooden stage.

"The theater? I didn't pay for a show."

Margaret's cheeks flushed to match the drapes. He strode past her into the room to explore what appeared to be recent work on the stage.

With his hands running roughly over the improvements, he heard her say something about Gregory redoing the stage to save Mary's life. Sounded dramatic. Fitting.

"Why are we in the theater?"

Margaret sighed. "We all used to put on these silly plays together."

"We?"

"You. Me. My brother, Gregory, and his now-wife, Mary. She used to write the most nonsensical, but whimsical tales. Now she has started quite the name for herself, but that's a story for another time." She paused, looking up at him. "Do you...remember?"

He felt that familiar sensation again, his essence, when he looked at her. Her eyes. That was all he heard. Eyes didn't speak, but hers did just now. And he heard them clearly. Her large, chocolate, almond shaped eyes, tucked away, spoke softly. He heard her asking him if it was okay that she probed. He heard her saying that she couldn't imagine his pain, and that she suffered too. He heard her saying that it was all going to be okay, that everything was fine right now, and that if at some point it wasn't fine in the future, they would manage that then.

Hearing too much, he shook his head. He couldn't make sense of the fact that he could hear her thoughts when he hardly knew her.

"What kind of plays?"

"Mermaids and pirates, of course!"

He raised a suspicious brow.

"You wouldn't believe me if I told you."

"That does seem to be our norm."

"Come." She threw her arms out to the sides as if to embrace the air and energy of the room, twirled once, clapped, and pranced through the doors.

His body followed, usurping his permission. Ostensibly, without the twirl, clap, and prance.

They made their way to the gardens. The autumn air held a refreshing chill, and the sun, when peeking from behind the clouds, offered a warm touch.

He watched her achingly round bottom take full shape as she bent to smell the few flowers left in bloom during the autumn season. The swift tightness in his pants caught him unexpectedly. Thoughts leaked into his mind of how it would feel for that apple-shaped bottom to rest between his thighs.

She whirled around and he was never more thankful for loose breeches.

Held in her hand where flowers with sporadic periwinkle petals joined to fuzzy yellow centers. "Do these mean anything to you?" She coyly asked.

"Should they?"

She laughed softly, "Not really. They're asters. They mean love and daintiness."

"Why would I know–"

Ignoring his question, she had already twirled back around and was bending over again. He groaned.

"What's that?" She turned her head over her shoulder and glanced at him under fluttering eyelashes.

"I was just asking–"

"Nevermind." She untwisted then unfolded her body and flung a handful of new flowers toward him, so lovely that artists ached to capture them. They were blood red, almost honeycomb-shaped petals, in a low dome shape. "These?"

"Nothing."

"They're dahlias. They represent good taste."

"I'm pretty sure you win the game. I wouldn't know a rose from a tulip. Or what either of them mean. What's the significance of this? Did we all used to send each other secret messages with flowers?" He chuckled. Surely, the inane plays were the extent of his ridiculousness with this woman.

"Yes! You remember!"

Shocked, he shrugged his shoulders. "Next you'll be telling me that Gregory and I taught you fencing and expletives."

Margaret's eyes widened.

Jonathan's eyes widened.

"Please tell me that's not true."

Margaret slowly nodded. She paused and cocked her head. Her eyes narrowed, and she whispered. "You must remember. Somewhere inside of you."

He hadn't realized that he stood within a hand's reach of her now as he listened to her eyes again. They were saying something so quietly that he couldn't hear the words. But whatever they were saying was pulling him closer to her. So close he almost reached out to put his hand on her trim waist. The waist that his hands remembered from his past life and wanted to explore more in this new life that he had been given.

He hadn't asked for this. This draw. This connection. He hadn't asked for any of this. Losing all his memories. Vaguely recalling others. His subconscious filling in gaps that made no rational sense. Who had he been before?

It didn't matter. This was now. Unfortunately right now, right here, he couldn't kiss her.

MARGARET COULD HARDLY BREATHE. She wanted Jonathan to kiss her. She wanted to lean in. She wanted his restless hand on her waist, migrating to the small of her back, drawing her in to him. She wanted to press her hands into his chest and confirm the strength she envisioned there.

When she had twirled around earlier with the asters in hand, she had noticed the tightness in his pants and the bulge that had been waiting for her. Waiting for her to back onto and sate. And, oh she would have sated it. Sated it with all she had.

But this was the garden. Where anyone could walk by at any moment.

And beyond that, memories from three years past banged on the gates of her heart. She hated how he left her the first time when she was eighteen. Before he went missing.

She had planned to show him a few innocent places around the estates that didn't hold any passionate significance for them, but it was impossible to look at Jonathan and be devoid of feelings. He stirred her.

Since she had emptied herself of all the emotions that had filled her soul because of him, they couldn't possibly return, she was sure of it, they were locked away. But today proved the fallaciousness of that line of logic.

Next time she would be more cautious. So she told herself.

Chapter 6

M ARGARET LAY IN BED sipping her chocolate. She stared past the floral canopy with its bed curtains tugged open at each of the four mahogany bed posts and scrutinized the wainscoted slate blue walls. Despite not being an individual prone to melancholic thoughts, she envied the straight lines and their perfect joints. If only life could be so neat. Alas, life, and all those in it, are uncontainable. Indefinable. Unpredictable.

Knowing she would face Jonathan soon automatically rerouted her thoughts to him. It should be easy to be cautious around Jonathan. Margaret knew she desired nothing less than to be someone's shining star, and Jonathan had long ago rejected any illusions of that happening with him. He had drawn the lines, she just wasn't within them.

She recalled their last kiss three years ago in her bedchambers making her want to press her abdomen into her mattress and put a pillow between her legs, as if anything could replace the hardness of his shaft against her aching need.

She remembered kisses and let her mind amble down through the memory she had staved off for so long.

"Maggie, you couldn't possibly make me want you anymore." Jonathan was lying next to her with his leg atop her, pulling her closer to him. As if she could be any closer. His breeches were not thick enough to disguise the size or heat emanating from him. Nor should they be.

She felt a surge of fire light, a column in her core, and arched into him, crushing her breasts against him. The steel of his rod was enfolded in her thighs.

"Johnny, trust me," she panted in his ear, "I'll make you want me so hard that you'll never want for anything again."

A low growl tumbled out of his throat. His body was begging for her. The power she had over his body was too much and the dizziness forced her to stay lying down.

"Make me yours," she pleaded. "Only yours." He tore at her dress while she continued her supplication. "And I'll make you mine." If she had known his secret, she wouldn't have continued prattling on with her pleas and promises. "We'll be one. Together. Always and forever."

Then he stopped. His head was bowed reverently between her still fully clothed breasts. She could feel the heat and moisture from his breath.

"I can't." He mumbled. "I'm sorry." He propped himself up on his elbows and dry-washed his face with his hands. "How did I let it get this far?" Smacking the mattress, he pushed himself up.

"God, Maggie, why?" He met her eyes for a brief second and then ripped his gaze away. "Why did it have to be you?" He mumbled.

"Johnny?"

"Please. Don't. I'm sorry. I never should have–"

"What's going on?" She knew to never ask a question she didn't want the answer to, but she truly, from the depth of her heart, thought she wanted the answer. She believed to the furthest extents of her soul that no answer to that question could make her shun him. Her spirit was bonded to his in a way that no sealant could compare to. So when he finally answered her question, she wondered when she would ever trust her heart, soul, or spirit again.

"I'm betrothed."

His utterance was a raspy whisper, but it was clear enough. Except it wasn't clear at all. If he was betrothed she would have known. She would have heard about it. He would have told her.

He was sitting up on the edge of her bed now.

"What do you mean?" She asked, certain she wanted, needed, the answer.

He shrugged his shoulders.

"Don't you dare shrug your shoulders at me. Bloody hell, Jonathan! What the devil are you doing with me? You dratted rake! Damn you."

She pushed him. He acquiesced to her intention and stood up.

"It's been arranged since birth." He shrugged again, as if to ease the burden. "I had hoped she would have married someone else by now, or cried off. There was no reason for her to hold out for the second son. But she has, lord knows why."

"I don't care about her. What about me? I'm ruined. What the hell, Jonathan?"

"I'm sorry."

"Your sorry means nothing. What are you going to do?"

"I can't do anything. It was arranged by my father since my birth. Something about a mutually beneficial match." He trailed off and shrugged again. "He signed the papers. I can't cry off. Her father would call me out. "

"What about me?"

"No one knows about us. You'll be fine. Gregory will take care of you. You have plenty of suitors."

Any thoughts that Jonathan was a gentleman had vaporized like a cloud. Had she ever truly known him? No. The man that had nearly been inside of her was a complete stranger.

"I'll ruin you." Margaret clenched her jaw under the hollow threat.

"You won't." He started to shrug his shoulders and caught himself. "If it makes you feel any better, give it your best shot."

But she hadn't been able to give it her best shot. Those were the last words he had spoken to her before he went missing.

And now he was here, amnesic, and the playing field was not even. He couldn't remember anything that had happened between them. Her body recalled everything. Even the fiercest competitor would not exploit an opponent under such conditions. She wasn't cruel.

No, she wasn't cruel. She wouldn't act on vengeance at all. Never had.

But she didn't have to be overly kind. Today she would just take Jonathan riding to see the folly. They wouldn't even have to talk if they were riding fast enough.

JONATHAN HAD WAITED IN the breakfast room weighing the odds of Margaret showing up or not. He marshaled his thoughts to strategize how best to extract whatever secrets Margaret was keeping from. He wasn't sure if today he would play the gentleman, the rake, or both.

He also wasn't sure if he would have won or lost his own bet, since Margaret appeared just as he was about to leave in search of her.

"I was just coming to find you," he noticed that her smile didn't quite have the reach he thought it normally had, and there was a sparkle absent from her eyes.

"Oh? Did we have plans for this morning?"

"None explicitly established."

He cocked an eyebrow.

"Just the expectations that I would show you around in hopes of triggering some memories."

"Yes, I suppose that is the unspoken obligation you have been burdened to undertake."

"'Tis no burden."

"Glad to hear it. What did you have planned for today?"

"Riding."

"Riding?"

"Riding."

"I went riding yesterday."

"Not with me."

"True..."

She huffed. Her eyes darkened and a cherry red flushed into her cheeks. Her rapid breath strained her breasts against her royal blue riding habit and urged his arousal to mirror the effect.

The breakfast room was the perfect place to resist such urges. "Lead on, Boadicea."

Her eyes narrowed, but she swiftly turned around and led them outdoors.

Henry greeted them at the stables.

"Nice to see you have a riding partner this morning, Your Grace." Jonathan noticed Henry wink at Margaret and wondered about its significance.

"Henry, please saddle Wildfire for me."

"Certainly, my lady." Henry sauntered off whistling a bawdy tune.

Margaret huffed again, but Jonathan wisely refrained from observing the physical aftermath. Gazing out to the estates, Jonathan asked, "Have you any destination in mind?"

"Perhaps."

"Ah, the delight of mystery."

She scowled at him. "You'll see it when you see it."

"Yes, that is the way of the eyes, isn't it?"

Exasperated, Margaret walked off in search of Henry, mayhap to admonish him for the wink he gave her earlier.

Once the two had saddled up, Margaret took the lead and Jonathan was content to follow, watching her slender back taper into that familiar trim waist. Perhaps content was the wrong word. Simmering with lust that at any moment might evolve into a raging boil was a much more accurate word.

Passing the pond, Jonathan called out, "Slow down."

Margaret pretended not to hear, even though she was only a few strides in front of him.

"Margaret?" He shouted too loud for her to ignore.

She turned her head and plastered a fake sweet smile on her face. "Yes, Jonathan?"

The fake sweetness pinched his gut. He much preferred her authentic self, and he'd take her ire and fire over this.

"What about the pond?"

"What about it?" She waited.

He waited.

"It's just a pond," she eventually ceded.

"Yet I feel drawn to it." He sighed. He couldn't understand the connection to the pond himself, how could he begin to share it with someone else?

Out of his periphery, he caught her head turn. He couldn't read the emotion she had masked. She had silenced her eyes. Whatever she was hiding, some of it had to do with the pond.

He shrugged his shoulders and heard a loud harrumph as he did so.

"It's just a pond Jonathan. Let's go." She took off in a gallop.

He had no choice but to follow until several minutes later she had finally stopped at a tall tower.

As he watched her fling herself off her horse, he thought he saw her wiping her eyes. Maybe some tears from the wind.

"It's the folly," Jonathan announced. "Of course, I remember this from when Gregory and Mary had their wedding here just at the end of summer."

"Wasn't it beautiful," Margaret had her arms outstretched and her head thrown back.

The sun was lingering on her cheeks, reluctant to move. He could feel the sparkle returning to her eyes more than he could see it.

"It is," he said more about her than the wedding. He had meant to use his rich, grown up, baritone voice, but instead the two words emerged from somewhere in his throat. He hoped she hadn't heard, or would at least pretend not to hear those two words, so he could try again.

But when she turned to him with her bewildered look, he knew his hopes were in vain. "It's so beautiful because my father built it for my mother as a symbol of love. It is a testament to love."

"So it is," he said with more depth to his voice this time.

"Should we climb to the top?"

"Of course," Jonathan grinned.

Upon reaching the top, the two were out of breath and nary an arm's length apart. She was smiling so brightly the sun was eclipsed. "I beat you."

He cocked his head. "To the top?"

"Yes, to the top."

"It was a race?"

"It always is," she laughed.

And his lips had to mirror hers. Their resounding laughter echoed off the crumbling walls. He couldn't remember the last time he felt so weightless, as if he was one of those ridiculously dangerous new hot air balloons from the continent.

"Has it always been?" He smiled at Margaret.

Chin tucked demurely, she answered sotto voce, "It has always been."

It was a calm quiet as the two rode around the estates and then headed back to the stables late that afternoon. Upon reaching the house, Margaret had offered to ring for some footmen to bring them a light repast in the garden.

The footmen had brought a blanket, basket, and several pillows.

"That was a perfect ride. Thank you for taking me to the folly."

Her smile produced a glow in his heart.

"It was nothing. I was hoping it might trigger a memory." Her eyes turned downcast as she continued, "But unfortunately it didn't help."

"It all helps." She looked up at him with rounding eyes encouraging him to speak. "Just being here has helped...I think." He chuckled. "It certainly hasn't hurt."

She looked down again and began to pour him a cup of tea.

"Cream and sugar–" he began to ask, but his voice caught as she interrupted him with two simple words that were really not so simple at all.

"I know."

The silence hung in the air as she presented the cup and saucer to him. It was so intimate. Just like the jacket he had instinctively adorned her with. He drew his brows together, wordlessly asking Margaret to share more.

She popped up to her feet. "Now I must change out of this uncomfortable riding habit. I bid you farewell."

And just like that, all of his innocent thinking flew through the gardens and he envisioned himself in her bedchamber helping her in her task. He would start by dragging the silk stockings down her thighs and would press soft kisses to each inch of skin as it was revealed...

Today he had been the gentleman again. He couldn't bring himself to make any untoward advances. Perhaps tomorrow the rake might have more luck extracting secrets.

Chapter 7

JONATHAN STOOD UNDERNEATH THE softly swaying leaves of the giant oak tree with his hand on the rough bark. "You want us to do what?"

"Climb it." Margaret smiled coyly in her dusty rose spencer and cream frock. The sun could not outshine her golden tresses, and those plush lips entreated him to kiss her. "We used to always climb trees together. Surely you haven't forgotten how to do it." That small smile hit him right in the middle of his chest. It was the glimmering light of life that so easily slipped from her lips that caught him unexpectedly and yet always welcomingly.

Jonathan eyed Margaret suspiciously. "And who would climb the fastest?"

"By now, you must know I won't give away those secrets." Her smile widened to encompass the skies and the sun's rays calling to his balloon-shaped heart to drift into her.

"The highest, then?" He teased, with a most charming half smile.

Her laughter trickled out of her and launched his heart into the air. "You silly man." She made a movement to swat at his forearm.

Using his quick reflexes, he pulled his arm back and clasped her hand within his own. Today he would be the rake.

MARGARET NOTICED SOMETHING WAS different about Jonathan today. Even when she had first seen him, she could tell that something had changed. Not his hairstyle, not his clothing, just something in his demeanor. His sharp jaw still accommodated a late day stubble, and his deep set eyes drank of life. There was an energy encompassing him that was drawing her in. She couldn't help swatting at him when he teased her for memories of climbing trees. Instincts had taken over.

But she couldn't let impulse win. She had to retain full control of herself to ensure she didn't leak the wrong memories to him.

His clasping hand was scorching, and not just where his skin was flush against hers. It was time to leave the danger of being on the ground next to this inferno and climb a tree.

She withdrew her hand, but not before he let his fingers feather down her wrist causing a small shiver in her core. Head high and eyes ahead, she strode to the tree behind Jonathan.

"What we need is a change of perspective."

"Is that what we need?" Jonathan's sultry voice was too close behind her, she could feel his breath on the nape of her neck, and all the hairs there stood to attention.

"Yes," she croaked through a dry throat.

Jonathan chuckled. "And climbing trees changes perspective."

"Being the more artistic of the two of us, you should trust me on matters relating to perspective."

"I wouldn't know."

She wanted to turn around and see if there were any emotions on his face. His voice gave away nothing. Instead, she turned her head and spoke to her shoulder, giving him her profile, "Yes, well, not including the obvious change in perspective, tree climbing offers a second change in perspective as well."

"And that would be?"

"You'll see."

With that she tugged up on her skirts and reached for the first branch. She felt the heat from Jonathan's hands surrounding her waist. "I'm fine. I've done this dozens of times."

"Yes, I'm sure you have..."

The hands squeezed tighter, increasing the heat and pushing it like a wave around her hips and down the valley between her legs.

She scooted up the first branch, leaving Jonathan behind. She didn't look back.

She particularly didn't look back to watch Jonathan take off his jacket. And she definitely didn't take notice of the strength bulging from his arms.

After a couple of grunts and huffs, she heard Jonathan behind her. He had caught up swiftly. "I feel like a child," he announced with a grin.

"Ah...And there you have the second perspective shift."

"Well, well, well, not just a pretty face then, are you?" He teased out a blush that she resented.

"Surely it didn't take climbing a tree to deduce that."

"Perhaps not." He ceded.

They had stopped climbing. She was one branch above him with her back against the trunk of the tree and her legs resting on the outward branch. Jonathan was half standing, half sitting. He rested with his back against the tree and one arm draped over a branch at chest height. One leg was holding himself up, and one leg was outstretched on a branch.

His head was near her hip.

"Based on my observations from today, I'm guessing I was the fastest."

"Definitely not." She crossed her arms over her chest. He would not goad her.

He laughed. "I would also *bet* that I always climbed the highest."

He had emphasized the fourth word, but Margaret missed the cue and focused on her winning argument, "I'm higher than you are right now."

He laughed and looked up into her eyes. "I bet I let you win." He winked.

He winked? What the–

Margaret was so startled at the subtle gesture accompanying the bait he put out, that she forgot she was in a tree. Leaning forward she lost her balance and felt the strong hands of gravity start to pull her down.

Only they weren't the hands of gravity, they were *his* hands. His blazingly hot hands, calloused from his time in the army and who knew what else. Yet tenderly and unyieldingly wrapped around her waist. She felt the iron bar of his forearm along the small of her back, clenched so tightly as if to ward off Thanatos himself.

"Steady. I have you."

And oh, did he have her. And she apparently had him. Her hands were tangled in his hair while her face was crushed against his cheek. Her eyes were welded shut, so her other senses were heightened. As if she needed a heightened awareness of her breasts pressed roughly against his solid chest and her honeypot nuzzled right up on his groin. Yes, she could feel it. And he was as hard as she was soft.

There was nothing safe to say at that moment. There was nothing safe to do. No safe way to move away, so she whispered into his jaw the only thing that had finally come to mind. "I thought you didn't make bets with ladies?"

"Not unless I know I'm going to win,"

"And are you going to win?"

He nudged his nose behind her ear, then down under her jaw to tilt her head. "I think I already have."

She felt the soft scrape of his stubble against her cheek, and then a warm, soft mouth pulling on her bottom lip. He paused.

As she felt his breath mingling with hers, she knew that she could stop him from going any further. She could refuse his delightfully wet invitation and push away. But her body would surely resent her more for rejecting the summons than accepting it.

She sighed and parted her lips. Against all odds, she pressed herself closer to him.

There was no restraint left. He darted his tongue into her mouth and she entangled herself in his. His hands roamed up her back and up along her ribs. She could feel his thumbs inching closer to the side of her breasts. *Yes, yes, yes.*

She rolled her heat over the bulge in his breeches and could feel the lightning surging within her. It wasn't enough to feel him rock hard beneath all these layers.

He groaned and pulled his mouth down her neck, nipping at her shoulder. His tongue trailed her decolletage and swept almost within reach of her nipple.

Oh my god! That tongue was about to wrap itself in her nipple, and if that happened she would lose all control.

"Jonathan,"

"Sweet, delicious, Margaret. You taste like peaches and custard."

"We're in a tree," she moaned.

"Hmmm... yes. Something about a change in perspective. I completely agree."

Amidst talking, he kept licking her breasts and now she was panting, heaving her breasts at him. They ached to be free of the layers and the dratted corset caging them in.

"Jonathan, I... you..."

"Mmm... I agree."

She needed to stop, but her body was begging for more. She rolled onto his arousal again and felt the heat swell in her body. It flooded her core and found release out through her limbs.

"Yes, Margaret. Take me. Use me. I'm yours."

"Johnn–Jonathan," she whispered. Her body went still. The throbbing, the humming, the aching savagely persisted. The relentless yearning to be with him and of him.

But she had to stop.

MARGARET HAD STOPPED. *Why did she stop?* Jonathan was as hard, as thick, and as long as the oak tree they had just climbed. He only wished Margaret had finished climbing him. But then again, maybe a tree wasn't the perfect place for this to happen. For their first time.

Jonathan slid his hands up and down Margaret's back. "It's ok, darling." He kissed her temple and into her hair while she rested her head against his chest.

Together they slowed their breaths until they matched inhalations and exhalations, deep and slow. Looking out into the small forest of trees that quietly enclosed them, he reflected.

His arms were wrapped around her, and she fit perfectly against his chest and in his lap. She brought out a character in him that he couldn't identify, someone light, carefree, even playful. Up until Margaret, the last three years had drudged along. He had resigned himself to not knowing anything of his past, and then one morning his mind breathed existence into the name Chatsworth.

If nothing else, coming to Chatsworth to discover Margaret was worth it. Her breezy, impulsive, yet determined nature, was calling something out of him. And he was desperate to answer the call.

"Shall we make our way down?" He nudged her hair with his chin.

"One more."

"Minute? Hour? Kiss?"

"Yes."

She looked up at him with endless depths. He could hear them asking for more of him.

Unsure of how to give of a unknown identity, he leaned down and gave the only way he could right now.

The second kiss was slower, deeper. It was a gentle swaying of bodies, swelling of breaths, and flirting of souls. There was no urgency. Time would wait for this kiss.

Chapter 8

T O MARGARET IT FELT like fourteen days rather than a mere fourteen hours since her kiss with Jonathan. She forced herself to stay distracted, at least for the morning, before answering the bellpull of her heart to go find him.

So she sat in the garden with her watercolors, painting some of the last aster and dahlia blooms of the year. Despite her impatience at times, painting often, like today, calmed her nerves.

Enwrapped in the decision between amethyst and aubergine, Margaret didn't hear the light tread on the gravel until the smooth baritone was directly behind her.

"Margaret," it sang. "Lovely day for painting."

The jolt from his voice flew up her arm and turned her aster into an aubergine.

She inhaled deeply and changed her paper to start again. Only, for the life of her, she couldn't see asters anymore, only aubergines.

"Yes, there are only a few weeks left of weather suitable for painting outdoors for the year. I thought I would take advantage."

"May I join you?"

She hesitated for only a second before the competitive side in her wanted to challenge Jonathan to a painting wager. Okay, she wasn't actually going to wager anything, but she still wanted to see his weight's worth in paint. "Alright. Have one of the footmen bring out an extra easel. Let's see what you can do."

"Haven't seen enough then?" His smile shone right through her heart, warming her inside out.

"Off with you, and don't dally." She waved her arm dismissively.

Placing himself in her direct line of sight, he teased, "Do I look like a dallier?"

The small gauntlet had been thrown, so she took it up by eyeing him slowly head to foot, "Most definitely."

He laughed as he strode off in search of a footman.

After fifteen minutes, Margaret observed Jonathan sitting stiffly with a brush in hand, staring at the blank sheet.

"The only way to know if you can paint is for you to try it."

"Yes, I'm just trying to find my muse." He paused to look around the garden. "Tell me, why do you paint?"

The question was innocent enough, but it caught Margaret unawares. Why did she paint? Because her mother had made her. Because her mother had paid for a tutor. Because it was what all genteel ladies did. Truly, Margaret could have stopped at any time. Why hadn't she?

There was a stillness to painting. To creating first in her mind what she wanted to produce on paper. There was a production to painting. To giving of and expressing herself through color. And there was a beauty to painting. To interpreting, crafting, and capturing a final image.

Aloud, she said, "It's quiet."

Their eyes met briefly, and she knew he was waiting to hear more from her. He wanted to listen to her, and for some reason that was enough of an argument to choose to open up to him.

"It stills my mind, if only for a short while."

"And then?"

"And then it's back to the madness dwelling here," she tapped her finger to her temple.

"It's a beautiful madness."

Margaret's cheeks warmed at the compliment but dismissed it, "Yes, well I enjoy the temporary asylum painting provides for a beleaguered mind."

Inwardly she cringed at her potentially insensitive comment to his condition.

He smiled reassuringly, "Then I'm sure I will take great pleasure in painting."

The two painted in comfortable silence until Jonathan winced and dropped his paintbrush.

"Ah," he let out a short burst.

Margaret flung her paintbrush down and pounded over to him. "What's wrong?"

Jonathan held two fingers to his forehead while his thumb massaged his temple. "I don't know. I just–Ah!"

"Don't move. Just wait here."

"No, please. I'm fine. I just feel like something is trying to wake up inside of my mind."

Margaret's hands were clammy as she tried to slow her breathing. "Are you sure?"

"Yes, I'm sure." He produced a lazy smile. "I'm glad to know you'd have such concern for me."

If only you knew. "Yes, well," and at that moment Margaret's eyes scanned what Jonathan had been painting. Flustered, she cast out a jumble of words, "Be that as it may, I'm just happy to know there is no concern to have to have."

Jonathan gave her quizzical look. "Are you okay?"

"Yes," she swatted the hand he was extending to her temple. "I'm perfectly fine. Everything is fine."

Everything was definitely not fine. Looking at Jonathan's painting, Margaret realized how close Jonathan might be to having a breakthrough.

All he had painted on his sheet was bubbles under water.

***

JONATHAN SAT IN THE library staring at the fire as the evening air chilled. He couldn't help thinking of the many layers of Margaret that he wanted to unpeel.

He thought back to the kiss in the tree. That kiss had fanned him into flame. Her eyes blew life into him. A life he couldn't comprehend or remember.

He knew she was hiding a past that they shared. But he didn't know why she wouldn't disclose the past to him. What had he done to her to deserve that? Or was it something she had done? Those were mysteries he longed to uncover.

Should he try to make up for it, without knowing anything of their past? Why remain silent? Why not just ask her? Was he afraid? If she divulged everything upon him asking, what good would it do if he didn't remember anyways? A heavy weight crept into his limbs at the thought of bearing a burden he couldn't own. Maybe there were some memories best left forgotten. At least for a time. Don't ask what you don't want to know.

This could be his chance to start anew with Margaret. Perhaps she wasn't telling him about their past because she had let it go. Why go dredging it up? Two parts coward, two parts respectful, and one part undecided, he would forge ahead and continue to cover ground.

MARGARET COULDN'T SLEEP. She wasn't looking for Jonathan. Not after she raided the kitchen for a glass of milk. Not after she scoured the study for a nip of whiskey. And certainly not when she found him in the library pouring over a book.

He must have been consumed by the words on the page because he hadn't yet looked up to acknowledge her.

Resting his cheek and jaw in the joint of his finger and thumb, she noticed he wore spectacles tonight, and she sucked in her breath. Jonathan had always been handsome, but seeing him now with his eyeglasses instantly made her nipples harden against her nightgown. He was a grown man with hair crawling out of his collar, thighs to ride, and an estate to run. How she wanted to crawl all over him, ride him thoroughly, and let her heart run away with him. But she must keep some wits about her. Some crawling, a bit of riding she would allow. If persuaded.

Without looking up, Jonathan spoke, "Although you are a woman of many talents, I doubt even you can read this from that distance."

If you only knew what I was reading right now.

He leaned back in his chair, and offered a half grin, "What can I do for you?"

Take off all your clothes.

"Ahem," she coughed more to clear her mind than her throat. "I didn't know you wore spectacles."

"I don't wear them often. Only when my eyes feel tired." He crinkled his brow and his eyes held an expression that she couldn't read. He took off his spectacles, and she moaned inwardly. "There's a lot you don't know about me, you know?"

"I wouldn't say a lot."

"I would."

She cocked her head. When he didn't continue, she began to tour the room, stalling to find the perfect place to sit. She chose the duchesse en bateau her father had imported from France as a wedding anniversary gift for his wife. Maybe if she kept her parents in mind, she could maintain her distance from him.

The silence had almost overstepped into discomfort when she said coyly, "You would, would you?"

"Yes, I would." Placing his palms on the table, he stood and stalked over to her. In a fluid motion, he straddled the piece of furniture and sat down, leaving her toes inches from his groin.

Real or imagined, she felt heat emanating from his thighs, and she yearned to stroke him with the pads of her feet. Before the image fully formed in her mind, he proceeded.

"How can you know me if I don't even know myself?"

"Because I've known you forever."

"You knew me before. But who am I now?"

"You're still Jonathan."

"Am I?" He inclined his head and his eyes roved over her body sending shivers down her chest into her groin.

Breathily, she answered him, "Yes."

"How do we know?"

"I know."

"That's not enough." Before she could interrupt, he continued, "What would the old Jonathan do?"

"I've told you."

"Some things."

"Some things," she repeated, staring into his eyes. "What more do you want to know?"

"I'm not sure what I want to know. I thought I wanted to know everything. Now, I'm not so sure. It's a strange condition to have no working memory, yet feel some things are familiar."

"Like what?"

"Like Chatsworth. Gregory. Riding horses. Pugilism." He paused, "You."

Margaret clung to the emotions rampaging out of her heart, full throttle toward Jonathan. She pressed one hand to her core, to hold herself together, as if with any sudden movement, or the perfect words out of his mouth, she might unravel and tie herself to Jonathan again. It was too easy to do so.

And then he was speaking again. "But," he added gravely. "What do I have to offer you? I can't give a self to you that I don't even know. There's no full self to give to you. You deserve a complete person, in their entirety, and absolute fullness." He rubbed his hands up his face. "I'm a shell of a person."

She couldn't help herself. Maybe if she had more discipline, she could have refrained. Maybe if she could hear the small voice of reason over the deluge of lust, she would have resisted. Maybe if she was an utterly different woman, not one so entwined with Jonathan's soul. But she wasn't. She didn't want to be. She couldn't be.

So she extended her foot, an extra few inches and grazed his inner thigh.

SPARKS FLEW FROM THE point where Margaret's foot touched his thigh all throughout his body. He knew he should hold back, but at the moment he couldn't remember why. All he knew was that she was here, wanting him. And he was here, wanting her.

"I don't even know the old Jonathan." He said as he slid his hand down his thigh onto her toes to warm her cold foot.

"That's okay. I do."

"So tell me. What would he do?" His hand flowed up her night-gown to her calf, and he heard a catch in her breath. He looked up to lust over her shuddering breasts. "Would he do this?" As his hand drifted up under her knee, he moved his whole body toward her until her legs were draped over his thigh.

Margaret dipped her head.

"And what about this? Would he do this?" He pushed himself as close as he could get to her. "And this?" He reached under her luscious bottom and pulled her to straddle himself. He could feel his arousal reaching toward her, almost touching her. And then she moaned. And all hell broke loose.

Her neck was a long, pale column, inviting him to draw his tongue up its endless length until he found her sweet taste of peaches, on her own tongue. She clashed her tongue against his.

"Jonathan," breathless, she pleaded, "Take me. Make me yours." He felt her nails digging into his shoulders, clawing for a way underneath his layers. Posthaste, he removed his cravat, jacket, waistcoat, and shirt.

It was a mistake. It was too much. Her fingers blitzed a wide swath all over his torso, and he was undone. He couldn't untangle himself from her limbs if he wanted to, thank God he most certainly did not want to.

And then he felt her press her bosom into his chest and he wished he could remove her nightgown. If he had known it was the night for wishes to come true, he might have dedicated more time to making them, but he didn't have time. He had now. And now Margaret had slipped out of her nightgown. She shivered against him, as if to burrow herself further into him.

He lowered his head and licked around her breast until he dipped further, heeding the directions from her moans, and took a nipple between his lips. He sucked, and she arched into him.

Holy hell, she was a goddess, purely formed and wholly formable under his touch.

Everything in him that he knew, and so much more that he couldn't recognize was drawing him to her. He needed her soft supple body crushed to him. He needed those long legs draped around him. He needed those lush lips pressed against him.

She was life, breath, passion, and everything he didn't know he had been needing so desperately. So he let a hand roam her body and explore her world. He pushed a hand gently into her hair and pulled back softly, opening her up to him more.

"Jonathan, touch me like only you know how to do."

Forgetting that he didn't know what she was expecting, he played on instincts and gently brought his thumb between her folds, to the holy nub waiting to blossom. She groaned into his mouth and took his tongue captive with her mouth.

Her moans mounted against him until she stole his breath with her panting and then returned it to him when she slumped against his lust filled body. Only, it was something a little bit more than lust now.

His soul felt bared before her, and he didn't care. It felt safe, despite the lack of answers. At least he had one answer.

Chapter 9

MARGARET COULDN'T DENY IT any longer. No matter where she sat looking at the Jonathan situation, her body would not allow her mind the covetous control it needed.

She had tried sitting and painting candidly at every angle of the drawing room until her mother, exasperated, told her to pick a seat and stay there. She had tried the angle a ways behind Lyle, watching Jonathan think about his next move, but all she imagined was him in his spectacles. With nothing else. So she tried the angle further behind Jonathan, but she couldn't think, nevermind paint, anything beyond his broad shoulders which she was sure bore the marks of her fingernails.

She needed his lips of today to kiss away any pain from the distant past still lingering. She pulled the corner of her bottom lip into her mouth, imagining the teeth sliding up over it to be his.

And even as she thought about his warm body against hers, she remembered his awareness of her body and mind. He was more than her adolescent sweetheart. He knew her for who she truly was, a zany chit with an eye for art and a heart to climb higher.

And a body to ride harder.

She extinguished the steaming thoughts from her mind and instead recalled the afternoon paint session they had enjoyed together. It had sparked more than just desire for him. Somehow it had triggered a memory in Jonathan, unfortunately one of the few memories Margaret didn't want him to recollect. For if he could remember that, he would remember everything that followed. Their whole blissfully happy then blindingly lost relationship.

There was one unexpected blessing that came from their encounter though. Since he had experienced a breakthrough of sorts, maybe she could use art to help others. Perhaps Margaret had accidentally sat through and discovered a new purpose she could pursue. If only she could be as courageous as her best friend Mary who became a playwright this past summer, she might find a greater purpose as well.

Ironically, Margaret was always considered the brave one. The social one. The impulsive one. The one waving her arms about, twirling around, and loosing twinkling smiles at all passersby. But could she chart a new course for her life? And on a whim, more or less?

The thought was to be taken up later because at the moment, Jonathan had stood up from the chess game and was stretching overhead. Nothing else mattered. Was there even anything else? She watched his long, solidly threaded arms arch into the sky and then come down to massage a shoulder.

Unawares, she began dragging her bottom lip into her wet mouth.

"Margaret," her mother softly reprimanded. "You're dripping."

Startled, Margaret's eyes flew to her mother's. Had she read her thoughts?

"Paint. On the Aubusson." And then as if talking to a child, "You're dripping paint on the rug, dear."

"Yes, mother. Thank you." She attempted to put her brush down without notice, but she caught Jonathan smirking at her. And perhaps when he returned to his chair he had sat back just a tad taller in his chair.

JONATHAN LEANED BACK IN his chair, itching for his imminent loss in the chess game.

"Jonathan," Lyle remarked, "I've won in 10 moves. Or 12, depending. I don't believe it's necessary to draw out the play, do you?"

"Hmmm? No." Of course it was entirely impudent of Jonathan to allow himself to be so distracted, but he couldn't take his eyes off of Margaret's bottom lip, especially when she kept nabbing it with her teeth.

"Very well. Good game." Lyle clapped him on the back and muttered, "Of sorts."

But Jonathan was too busy watching Margaret recover from her dripping paint to notice. God, she was remarkable. Unflappable. And entirely unashamed.

"Do you want me to ride you?"

He cocked an eyebrow at her. She hadn't said what he thought she said. She couldn't have. Could she?

"Mother suggested you may wish for some exercise. Do you want me to ride with you?" Margaret repeated coyly.

He cleared his throat. It was imperative. "Yes, the exercise will do us good."

As the two made their way out of the room, he could only maintain propriety for as long as they were within ears' reach of the parlor, and then he chased her as she flounced down the corridor, laughter trailing behind them.

When they had saddled up at the stables, Margaret took one second to secure his attention and then announced, "To the old fishing hole."

Having no idea where that was, perforce he galloped after her. And as he did, he imagined breathing in her jasmine scent. She was life itself. The embodiment of fullness and joy. Whoever he was now, he was going to give himself to her.

The wind blew through his mind, clearing his thoughts until the only image left was Margaret's backside in motion with the galloping horse ahead of him.

"Yah!" He called to encourage the horse to catch up with his riding partner.

He finally matched her stride as they slowed near a riverbank. Margaret flung herself off the horse and Jonathan followed, dropping the reins below the horse's neck thus commanding the horse to stay.

Margaret had already taken off her shoes and was sitting on the bank as she dipped her toes in the water. Jonathan reached for his temple as a vague memory fought its way to the surface. But he only saw water. It was the same vision as the first one he had while painting with Margaret. Bubbles underwater. Without any context, Jonathan couldn't decipher the puzzling picture.

Having taken off his shoes, he sat beside Margaret with his feet in the water as well.

He leaned back on his elbows. "What is it about water?"

Margaret whipped her head around to him, and tried to disguise her astonishment. "Water?"

He grinned. "Yes, water." He pulled her down to rest on his chest. "I used to walk around a pond back in Glaston. It held no significance to me, that I can trace. And since I've come to Chatsworth, the large pond has been calling to me every day."

She murmured a feigned curiosity.

"The ponds. The painting." He felt her slightly stiffen at the last word. "You saw it?"

"Yes," she drew out the word.

"Tell me."

"I can't."

"What can't you tell me? Why can't you tell me?" He pushed himself to sit up, and she curled her knees under her dress.

"I just can't."

"You can tell me anything."

She paused. "I think that may be true." Stalling, she pushed back a few loose blonde tendrils. "There are some things I just can't tell you." Her eyes pleaded with him. He could see the fear in them. How could he deny her this one request that she had of him, to keep a secret? It was only one small request. One small request that tore at his heart, yet he didn't know why.

He couldn't drop it. "Please, Margaret. Tell me."

She stood up in a huff. "I can't just tell you, Jonathan. It's too much. I'm afraid. You must know that we had a past. You're allowed to forget it. Why can't I?"

"Allowed?" He jumped to his feet. "Allowed?" His voice was growing louder. "This is not something someone permitted, besides the almighty in his great, unfathomable wisdom." The sarcasm was dripping from him. "It's not as though I asked for permission and he granted my request."

"Don't be ridiculous, Jonathan. And don't mock. It's unbecoming on you." He watched her plop her hands on her hips.

"You can't possibly think I want this."

"Maybe forgetting isn't so bad."

He heaved a sigh. He wanted to hug her. He wanted to shake his memories out of her. And then he wanted to hold her until she didn't have any more fear. "It couldn't have been that bad."

"You don't even know." Her voice trailed off, "You never did." Tears that were threatening to spill retreated at the sound of her voice, "And you never will, Jonathan. Do you hear me?" She marched off in the direction of the horses.

Well, one horse. The one horse that was still standing under the tree was the one with the reins hanging down.

"Blast it all to hell!" Margaret directed her invectives to the sky.

Jonathan had so many choices at that moment. He could have pitied her poor luck. He could have scolded her for her folly. He could have raged back at her and left her to walk home. He could have berated himself for past actions that had hurt her. Or he could laugh.

He could laugh because he wanted her to laugh too. He wanted to feel the lightness in her spirit and see the sparkle in her eyes. He didn't want to dwell on pain.

And since she was his muse, his joyous, full of life, impulsive and imperfect goddess, he barked out a laugh.

MARGARET WAS ENTIRELY DISPLEASED at Jonathan's roar of laughter. The least he could have done was leave her alone in her misery and misfortune.

Instead he was wiping tears of laughter from his eyes. The next second his hands were around her waist, thrusting her onto the saddle. Then he leapt onto the horse behind her.

"Margaret, my sweet, peaches and custard, Margaret," he breathed into her ear. "You are a delight." She squirmed under the tickling breath.

She crossed her arms and harrumphed.

Jonathan belted out another laugh.

"Not in my ear, if you please." She tilted her head up to the sky.

"Then where?" he said as he nuzzled the nape of her neck.

She would not break. The man was insufferable. Laughing at her affliction. What an abominable creature.

But that creature was all heat. All solid heat behind her. And when she had squirmed earlier, she swore she had felt his reaction.

So now she would make him pay.

Margaret arched her back, coaxing her bottom to rub onto Jonathan's groin. She could feel his arousal jutting toward her. "It's a good thing one horse stayed. It's a long way back."

Raspily, he voiced, "I left the reins down. Didn't you?"

"Oh, *that* you remember to do."

He lashed his arm around her torso. "You, Peaches, should hold your tongue."

"Or what?"

"I'll find a way to hold it for you."

Her breaths started coming in rapidly. She needed to regain control.

She leaned forward to brush the horse, pushing her bottom back into him, and talking sweetly to the horse. "What a good boy. At least *you* know how to do the right thing."

Hearing a half stifled groan, she pushed further back and extended her arm to pat the horse's neck. "Yes, you're a good boy."

"Is that what you want, Peaches? A good boy?"

Her nipples instantly hardened against her stays as she sat up. She writhed her bottom up onto his swelling arousal. "I want whatever you're giving."

She pushed her right shoulder into his chest and inclined her head to the left, exposing her neck.

He plundered her shoulder and the side of her throat. Then his hands were sweeping up her ribs, on both sides. The ambush forced her head back into his chest and his grands palmed her breasts, one in each gloriously warm massage.

"Jonathan," she throbbed. Her hands flew behind her head to grasp his hair, pulling him closer. It wasn't enough. She withdrew one hand and grabbed his thigh, feeling his fiery strength.

"Yes, Peaches?" He teased.

"I need you. Now Jonathan, damn you."

Jonathan stopped the horse and threw the reins overhead, dismounting in one fell swoop. The horse stood perfectly still as he grabbed Margaret, pulling her tumbling down into the long grass.

In all of this, he was a blur to her, but she knew he had removed any trace of levity from face. His hands were on her waist again. This time he was twirling her around to straddle him. His lips were all over her neck and then burning trails all the way down her chest.

Her skirts were up to her hips, and he had placed her cunny right on top of his shaft. Keeping the layers of clothing between them, he pulled her close. One heated hand was under her bottom, and the other had a vice grip on her hip. He was moving her inches at a time, back and forth over his hard length. Every movement was excruciating pleasure.

"There, Jonathan. Yes. Yes."

"Come for me, darling."

The tingling sensations overtook her body and white blinded her closed eyes. "Always," inaudibly broke from her lips.

Jonathan growled into the sky with his head thrown back, molding her against his body. He was pure man. Red-hot, growling, fully himself, and fully man.

Chapter 10

THAT MORNING, JONATHAN INCREASED his efforts to appear engaged in the monotony of playing chess. At the moment, his index finger was over his mouth to convey a pondering posture, when in fact it was shrouding a yawn.

Bugsby glided in the room carrying a tray with a calling card. With a bow, he offered it to Jonathan.

Straining to stifle jumping from his seat, Jonathan reached for the card. "Dr. Walker? Well, I'll be. I wasn't sure he would make the trek. Please show him in."

"Yes, Your Grace." And within a few short minutes, Bugsby was announcing Dr. Phillip Walker to the drawing room.

Jonathan sauntered over and clasped the doctor's hand in his, despite the norm to refrain from physical displays of sentiment. And then, just to truly flaunt the norm, he drew the nonplussed doctor into a one arm hug with a pat on the back.

"So glad you could make it Doc." Jonathan turned to Lyle, gesturing to Dr. Walker, "This is the man who saw to my sanity and even welcomed me into his own home."

Lyle stood and dipped his head, "I've heard much about you. It's a pleasure to finally meet you Dr. Walker."

"The pleasure is mine."

"I believe the game Jonathan and I were playing was nigh finished, and I was just about to take my leave for some exercise. I'll leave you two to catch up, and I'll see you this evening, I'm sure."

"Yes of course."

As Lyle left the room, Jonathan repeated his elation at having the doctor here at Chatsworth.

"How could I decline a short stay at such an estimable estate?" He returned the pat on Jonathan's shoulder. "So Jonathan, my boy, you now have a name, hmm?" The lack of proper ducal address failed to offend Jonathan given the doctor's avuncular disposition and mutual affection. "And some pieces are starting to come together to shape for you an impression of who you were. How is everything settling for you?" The doctor tapped his head, "In here?"

"Well, I haven't quite woken up yet," Jonathan jested. "But I sure hope it happens sooner rather than later."

"Time is in other hands, my boy."

"So it would seem."

"Good hands, but unpredictable. It's our greatest achievement to yield to the hands of time and our greatest satisfaction to think we've beaten it."

"Ever the philosopher, what?"

"Truer words...and such."

"Yes, well, they are indeed words steeped in yards and years of experience."

Dr. Walker chuckled. "While I haven't traveled too many yards beyond Glaston, but I do believe my years make up the deficit."

Jonathan grinned at the old man. In spite of having known him for only a few years, he was currently the most familiar face on the planet to him, and there was something peaceful about having him around.

"Have any memories come back?"

Jonathan's lips steeled in a line. "None specifically." He rubbed his hands up his face. "Just the water."

"Ah, they have a pond here too that you've walked more than the locals?"

Jonathan grinned. "It's been mostly sitting and meditating here. But yes, they too have a pond." Jonathan inhaled, "And there was also an incident with painting."

"Hmmm...painting."

"Yes," Jonathan hesitated.

Dr. Walker waited silently, comfortably, with his hands clasped in his laps. Bugsby must have anticipated Jonathan's requirement for tea, because at that moment, two footmen came in carrying tea trays and sweets.

There was no specific memory to share with the doctor, only a vague sensation that water, specifically the pond at Chatsworth, could potentially unlock the flood of memories waiting behind the dam in his mind.

"Margaret invited me–rather, I invited myself–to a painting session out in the gardens. At most I thought it could trigger a memory, and at the very least I..."

Jonathan didn't want to finish the thought.

"...Could spend time with a pretty young lady?" Dr. Walker finished for him with a grin.

Why did Jonathan feel embarrassed to say the truth? He wasn't a young lad sneaking kisses, he was a grown man, expected to have experience. Experiences.

But perhaps he wanted the one man who *knew* him to give his approval. Would he approve? Jonathan wasn't sure he approved himself. His actions could singularly ruin Margaret and there was no turning back. If he had any ethics, he would offer for her. But he couldn't marry her. Could he?

And just then Margaret swept into the room bringing a glow and warmth that he hadn't realized was missing. Her eyes sparkled upon acknowledging him. He caught his breath.

This woman knew him better than he knew himself. It was quite possible that she knew him better than any person at any point in time ever had. His own family would never even have had a chance to catch up to her.

Wordless, he watched as Margaret approached. He forgot that Dr. Walker was standing beside him. He forgot that he was standing in Chatsworth. He forgot that he had forgotten everything, and all he remembered was Margaret. Light and life. Sparkling joy. What would it be like to be immersed in her?

"Ahem," the doctor was clearing his throat.

Jonathan looked back and forth between Margaret and Dr. Walker. Then back and forth between them again. "Oh yes, quite. Lady Margaret, this is Dr. Walker." Margaret curtsied. "Dr. Walker, Lady Marget."

"The painter?" Dr. Walker murmured, though not quietly enough.

Margaret beamed, and her smile tugged at his heart. Jonathan grinned like a schoolboy given extra sweets at Christmas.

The doctor cleared his throat again, mumbling, "Must be something in the Chatsworth air." He glanced at Jonathan. Then Margaret. And then waited.

Then deciding he had waited long enough, Dr. Walker severed the silence. "Jonathan mentioned that you paint."

"Yes, I enjoy painting. It clears the mind," she spun a glance toward Jonathan, "Until it doesn't." He couldn't help giving her a crooked grin. "But usually it does."

"Yes. Clearly," the doctor chuckled to himself. "Might you join us for some tea?"

"Certainly." She grinned at the doctor. "There's nothing I love more than a spot of tea." She winked at Jonathan, and he had to rub his hand over his chest to quiet the mounting tattoo.

"I was telling the doctor about the water I painted," Jonathan disclosed.

"Oh?"

"We didn't dive too deep into it," the doctor chuckled at himself. Once he regained his composure, he continued, "I was going to suggest to Jonathan that we might try painting again. Perhaps therein lies a key to the door of his memories."

Jonathan couldn't read the expression on Margaret's face, when out from behind her temporary mask came the most angelic glow he had ever witnessed.

"Do you think?" She said eagerly. "Do you really think that painting might unlock some memories? I had an inkling, but I couldn't be sure. You could be sure though. You're a doctor. If only you could observe it happening, mayhap you would have some insight to share. Wouldn't that be grand?"

"Just grand," Jonathan teased.

"Oh shoosh." Margaret casually swatted her hand in his direction. "Dr. Walker, do you think that if it works for Jonathan, painting might be beneficial to others in a similar condition? Perhaps offering a breakthrough for others?" Margaret had edged herself so close to the last inch of her seat, Jonathan wasn't sure how she was sitting upright. It must be the sheer adrenaline in her legs holding her stable.

"I do believe with some observation, we could make some conjecture on the possibilities. It wouldn't be pure speculation, but there is not much research in the way of amnesia, so any hypotheses are better than none at this point."

Margaret clapped her hands together and pushed herself to the back of her seat. She proceeded to tap her index finger against her chin. "I wonder..." she murmured to herself.

Jonathan had never seen her so ebullient. Well, he had. But that was a different kind of happy.

"It is decided then. You must observe Jonathan. And we must paint. And then you must observe him some more to see if there are any changes. The more observation, the better!" Margaret's grin was so contagious that Jonathan hadn't comprehended what he was smiling about and agreeing to until he took a sip of tea.

If Dr. Walker was always around, when would he *not* be?

Jonathan immediately began gathering all the data in his mind that would lend to him successfully foraying into Margaret's bedchambers post daylight.

MARGARET'S EXCITEMENT WAS GUSHING out of her, reflecting on how her painting hobby might possibly give her the purpose she had been craving. If painting could potentially help sick patients, she would be more than willing to start a society offering this service. It could be The Society of Arts and Painting to Aid Mental Instability. Ok. The name needed work.

Jonathan might just be her muse.

And now she looked at Jonathan. My God. He had displayed the most lopsided grin earlier that had melted her heart. Now he sat more pensively, and she wanted to launch herself onto him. To hug him. To hold him. To squeeze the studious look off his face. She wanted to be as close to him as humanly possible. It wasn't wanton. It wasn't a burning between her legs. It was a burning and aching in her heart. It was...She shook her head. She didn't know what it was.

But whatever it was, she wasn't going to let it walk out the door and leave for three years.

"Dr. Walker, did Jonathan even offer you a chance to rest after your long journey? I fear he has been a terrible host." She shook her finger at him and winked discreetly.

"I do say he is an excellent host, all things considered." Dr. Walker chuckled, "But I am gaining in years, more than in pounds thankfully. And I believe I could use a rest."

"I'll have Bugsby see to a room for you."

Margaret rang the bellpull and made arrangements for Dr. Walker to repose in a guest bedchamber.

The instant she was alone with Jonathan, she whirled around to him. A few paces away, he stood in front of his chair because she had risen to see Dr. Walker off. She watched him standing there clueless of her intentions, and she stalked over to him. Thrusting her finger at his chest, she pushed him down into his chair.

He plopped down and grinned up at her. His arms hung casually over the arms, and his legs were spread wide.

"Yes, Peaches?"

She tapped her finger against her chin. "Hmm...whatever shall I do with you?" as she stroked his body from groin to lips with her eyes.

He reached for her wrist, and she playfully pulled it away.

"No one's here," Jonathan asserted, trying to nab her other wrist but to no avail.

"My mother is still around, somewhere."

"All the more fun," Jonathan's eyes gleamed as he pushed himself forward in his chair, only inches from her torso.

"Fun or...folly?" Margaret exclaimed the last word as she twirled around and ran for the door, just out of his grasp.

She made it two paces from the door before he was behind her with his forearm belted around her waist. She could feel the rapid movement of his chest against her back and the warm puffs of breath on her neck. Her own breathing was in doubletime to his, and she unconsciously separated her legs to allow him to slide his leg between hers. Now she could feel the solid, sheer muscle pulsating against her groin as she eased down onto him.

She ached for him to tear her dress off her shoulders and rip open her corset to suckle her breasts. But this was not the place.

"Jonathan," her hoarse voice mustered. "My bedchambers. Now."

She grabbed his forearm, unleashed herself, and ran out the door with no idea how to make this impulsive suggestion work.

Chapter 11

MARGARET DIDN'T MAKE IT back to her bedchambers. She didn't make it hardly twenty paces until she was waylaid by her mother calling her. Apparently she was in dire need of Margaret's help for the house party she was hosting for the week.

"Margaret, you nearly bowled over me. What is the rush?" her mother blew some stray hairs away with a puff of air. Her mother looked a tad disheveled. She was never disheveled. Every hair had a place and knew it. Margaret's lips parted to speak but were interrupted by her mother. "Oh nevermind, I'm glad you nearly ran into me. I need your help. I was just on my way to find you."

Steadying her heart rate and her voice, Margaret aimed for polite curiosity, "What do you need me for?" It came out a bit more mildly ruffled than she intended.

Her mother was certainly distracted, for she didn't perceive the peculiar tone. "Come. We have some preparations to make for the guests' arrival and dinner this evening." She put her arm through

Margaret's and led her to the kitchen to what Margaret could only imagine would be for discussions on the evening's menu. They hadn't much time left before the meal, so Margaret was largely decided that the menu wasn't capable of many changes; however, seeing her mother in even somewhat disarray charged her to provide any assistance she could.

As they strolled toward the kitchen, Margaret heard her mother muttering about cold meats and fish stew. Then, more audibly, she deciphered something about how, "...they are all coming this evening."

"Forgive me mother, but it must have slipped my mind. Who is all coming this evening?"

"Our regular guests. The Earl of Winchester and his family. Colonel Hastford."

"And Dr. Walker."

"And Dr. Walker," her mother mindlessly echoed. Then she tugged on Margaret's arm and they jolted to a stop. "Dr. Walker?"

"Yes, he arrived earlier this morning."

"Well, then I must ensure we set an extra plate." The dowager duchess dropped her jaw and brought her fingers over her mouth. "Oh dear, and I forgot your cousin was coming to stay as well."

"Which one?"

"Bella."

Margaret gasped. "Truly?" Bella was Margaret's favorite cousin, a free-spirited-down-to-earth woman she could trust with anything.

Her mother, not one to be exasperated, exhaled slowly, "Yes, truly."

The confirmed information gave Margaret cause to twirl and embrace her mother. "It's been too long!"

"It's probably been only several weeks. I'm sure she was at Gregory's wedding."

"Yes, well that's several weeks too long. Oh! She'll just love what's growing in the orangery since her last visit." Margaret released a short squeal.

Her mother chided her, "Really, dear. Must you?"

"I must." Margaret clapped her hands together. "Now let's go plan this dinner."

After negotiating with Cook for a meager ten minutes, only to have Margaret's earlier suspicions confirmed, it was with great concession and no small amount of disappointment that the dowager duchess agreed to the fact that the menu indeed could not be altered too drastically. The plate settings, however, were still up for discussion.

At that time Margaret had slipped away in fanciful hope Jonathan was waiting for her. He was not.

If Margaret had known that she wouldn't find time to be alone together with Jonathan for at least one busy but hollow chunk of twenty four hours, she might have tried harder to see him. But as it were, not only had the number of footmen seemed to increase, but their alertness had amped up to high with a new guest in the house and more on the way.

So without Jonathan physically around, Margaret took her time fantasizing about him instead. She had known how easy it would be to fall for him. Not that she'd yet fallen for a second time. That was why she guarded her heart so closely when he first came back. But somehow her soul was tied to his. Intricately. Indelibly. Perhaps interminably.

She thought of his cheeky grin. Although it had changed from before, he was still uncannily the same man. The man who challenged her, amused her, aroused her. To passion. To paint. To help others. To be her true self. Hiding nothing. Apologizing for nothing. He accepted that, like water, she was powerful, striking, immersive.

As she fantasized, she allowed Adeline to spend extra time on her dress and hair for dinner. The result was an exuberant lady's maid, a proud mother, and a delicious look from Jonathan that evening.

JONATHAN STOOD, DRINK IN hand, waiting for the dinner call. He felt somewhat unprepared for a more formal dinner gathering, but he still wrapped a smile on his face and extended as warm a welcome to the new arrivals as he could muster.

Later, feeling a touch uncomfortable around people whom he didn't remember but who knew him, Jonathan casually attached himself to Dr. Walker's side. For the doctor's sake, of course.

Then he saw Margaret enter the room in her sky blue dress with a flowery lace covered bodice that trailed down the tops of each large pleat outlining her slim waist and swelling bosom.

He was eager to sit next to her and whisper to her over dinner. Only, he didn't sit beside her. Or across from her. The dowager duchess adhered to a table etiquette he didn't have any interest to decode and which placed him a couple seats down and across from her.

At least he could still see her wide open sky mien and sparkling eyes. Until he couldn't because Colonel Hastford was sitting to his left, blocking his view. Even he knew it would be rude to attempt a conversation with her at this distance. If only he could just catch her eye.

"It's good to have you back, Your Grace." The Colonel pulled him out of his pining.

"It's good to be back. It's been too long."

"It has. Much has changed."

"Indeed. That is quite the understatement." Jonathan had trouble staying focused and coming up with a new topic to add to the conversation. "I think–" He heard Margaret's laugh ring out for all to hear, and he pondered the source of it.

"You were going to say?" Colonel Hastford prompted when Jonathan didn't pick up his thought.

Jonathan gazed past the Colonel, deaf to his question.

Without hearing a word of the conversation unfolding at Margaret's corner of the table, he was still quite certain he had interpreted the chatter. Since Margaret was grinning all ears, she must be discussing her new project and how painting might be able to help others. He was glad for her. More than glad. His heart was light. Floating on air for her happiness. Come to think of it, he was particularly interested in her suggested therapy, especially after some of the torturous methods he had heard of for treating mental conditions. He thanked God he had been deposited at Glaston with Dr. Walker rather than someone else who may have tried a more punitive approach to trigger brain repairs, as was the more common practice by leading physicians.

As Margaret grew more animated in her discussion, he noticed the table was steadily declining in formality, and ears were prickling to listen in.

Miss Katherine, true to her impulsively and impolite nature, was the first to lean into the conversation with what appeared to be a genuine curiosity, "A society for painting? What would you do?"

"We would set up paints and easels and facilitate a space for patients to paint."

"So you would visit asylums?" the Countess of Winchester couldn't help joining in, albeit dubiously.

"We could visit them or create our own building with our patients."

"That would be quite the undertaking," Dr. Walker chimed in. "But if anyone can do it, I believe it would be you."

Margaret beamed at him. She was surprised at his confidence in her, but she supposed that it spoke as much to the doctor's character as it did to her own. Afterall, he was the one who had been overseeing Jonathan's progress since his accident.

"How could you possibly know?"

"Just a feeling," Dr. Walker tapped his heart.

It seemed as though everyone was joining the conversation, so Lyle had no qualms in adding across from the table, "If McAdam can revolutionize roadbuilding by next year through macadamization, surely you can find someone to design and construct you a common building. Or perhaps simply find one for you to lease or buy."

Jonathan mistakenly overheard Miss Agatha whisper to her sister, Lady Cross, "Macadamia? I wonder how those nuts the sailors are bringing back from Australia would help in road construction."

Lady Cross mumbled something indistinct while Bella coughed. Or choked out a chuckle. He thought he saw Margaret exchange a glance with Bella, but he couldn't be sure.

From there the conversation turned to the feasibility and probability of raising roads and using gravel for drainage while Jonathan continued to discreetly observe Margaret. The rising and falling of her breasts with each breath was enough conversation for him, but at some point he knew he would have to make a trifle more effort.

He felt eyes on him and looked up to briefly catch the dowager duchess's eyes on him.

That was the only kick in the breeches he needed as a reminder to make more conversation with his mouth and less with his eyes.

***

A FULL TWO COURSE dinner passed from leek and ham soup and fricassee of chicken to braised beefsteaks and culminating with pudding. The men took port while the women made their way to the drawing room for tea.

When Jonathan could finally enter the drawing room with the other men, he made a point to restrain himself from making a direct beeline to Margaret. She was gracefully playing the pianoforte as Miss Agatha turned pages for her.

Maybe he could convince the younger sister, Miss Agatha that she needed a break. Afterall, turning pages was an onerous mental task, and, well, Miss Agatha appeared to have limited abilities, mentally.

Said persuasion was as easy as Jonathan's prognostication, and soon he was a hair's breadth from her silky skin. There was a card game at hand along with multiple conversations entertaining the guests more than Margaret's music, so Jonathan chose this moment to whisper discreetly. "You have quite the predilection for various artistic endeavors, Lady Margaret. Or should I say, artisan? Might you be a multipotentialite?"

"Is that a proclivity for sesquipedalianism I detect? Perhaps you feel threatened and are competing with big words against me and my multiple potentials."

"I daresay I should like to personally partake in these potentials."

"I believe that could be arranged."

"Shall we say, gardens? Midnight." He whispered into her ear. It took all of his willpower not to end the whisper with a nibble on her lobe.

The hour hands trodded slowly to midnight, and patience was not Margaret's strong suit. At half past eleven, she made an excuse to leave the gathering due to a headache. The party would likely be breaking up soon enough, so she was sure no one would notice.

Jonathan commanded himself to wait for at least one other guest to leave before he followed Margaret. Thankfully the doctor excused himself, due to fatigue, and Jonathan leapt on the opportunity to make his departure as well. Surely a young man of eight-and-twenty could be as tired as a septuagenarian.

Once he reached the doors to the garden, Jonathan was bounding down the pathway until he found Margaret at the fountain where they had painted together. He whisked her into his arms and pulled her down onto the grass.

She squealed as he began nibbling on her lobe the way he longed to do back in the drawing room.

"Jonathan," she melted into his arms and wriggled around until her body was pressed against his. As she wrapped her fingers into his hair, he thought about the incongruency between her perfection and his imperfection. She was whole, full of life, and unscathed. He was a shell, often finding himself clinging to joy. But she was his joy, and he would cling to her for now.

It could have been five minutes or an hour that passed between his thoughts and their kisses when he heard, "They must be here somewhere." The voice was indisputably Miss Katherine's.

The impertinent chit. What was she doing here? Jonathan couldn't spare merciful thoughts toward her at the moment.

Then the crunching of gravel was all too near. He could hear someone kicking pebbles. Once struck him on the cheek. He muffled an "Ow."

But it wasn't muffled enough. Bella, the pebble-kicker, was there in one stride bent over Jonathan and Margaret.

"Margaret?" Bella hissed.

"Uh, hello cousin."

"Quick! Get behind the bushes. Everyone will see you if you don't."

It didn't take Jonathan more than a trice to jump up and sweep Margaret into his arms and pull them both behind the bushes. Breathing hard, he held her tightly under his body. If he hadn't known a slew of people were soon approaching, he would have given into the hardness thickening between his legs.

He gave Margaret a quick kiss, and then a "Shh," as they waited, lying breathless in the dark.

"I swear," it was Miss Katherine again. "They both must be out here. Leaving within fifteen minutes of each other. Don't they have any sense? I'm surprised her mother isn't out searching for her."

"They weren't the only ones who left the room, you know," Lady Bainsbury, Katherine's older, more timid sister Charlotte touted.

"Yes, well an eighty year old doctor has a right to go to sleep at midnight. I'm surprised he lasted that long," Katherine rebutted.

"Anyone for another swig?" Lord Reginald Bainsbury, the eldest of the three, was holding up a bottle of whisky.

"I don't know why you brought that out here, Reggie?" Katherine chided.

"It's for the men," Viscount Ingleby taunted as he drank from the bottle. "Right, Colonel?"

"Quite." Colonel Hastford passed the bottle along to Lyle who took a sip and passed it back to Reggie.

"You just wouldn't understand manly things, Kat." Reggie poked his sister in the shoulder. Or at least, he tried to. It was more air than shoulder, as it was more alcohol than blood in his system. "Manly things like drinking, betting, building."

Kat belted a laugh. "Drinking, check. Betting, check. Building? What do you build, Reggie?"

Affronted, Reggie puffed out his chest, "Look here now, Mr. Fairfax and I will be investing in macdam...madam..."

"Macadamization," someone supplied.

"Madamization" Reggie slurred with his finger pointing high in the air, "Next year will be a big year. 1816. Mark it down. The year of the roads. You'll see."

"Whatever, Reggie," Kat rolled her eyes. "As if you know anything about engineering. Or investing for that matter."

"I know plenty. Nevermind you," Reggie set his sights on another means of approval. "I can see discussing manly things is better with manly men."

He threw his arm over Colonel Hastings shoulder, and whispered. At least, he thought he whispered, "How about Margaret this evening in that dress?" With his free hand he drew a sloppy version of her curves. "She's always been on my prigging list, but tonight pushed her to the top of it."

Margaret shivered causing Jonathan to stiffen. If he had heard Reggie's insolent comment, so had everyone in the vicinity. He was protecting Margaret beneath his body, but at the moment he felt like he wasn't protecting her at all. Sure, he would save her from ruin by hiding her from the troop a few feet away, but he had encouraged the assignation in the first place. Now he was hovering over her, completely incapable of defending her honor lest he ruin her reputation, and future, in the act.

"That's enough," Colonel Hastford gripped Reggie's arm and twisted it behind his back. "Being three sheets to the wind is no excuse. You'll have the decency to behave like a gentleman in the presence of ladies." When Reggie made no comment, the Colonel brought Reggie to his knees. "Apologize."

"I'm sorry!" Reggie squeaked out.

"And you'll have the integrity to speak properly about a lady, lest I call you out. Lady Margaret is beauty personified and to degrade her using such disregard is dishonorable."

"Yes, you're right. I apologize."

In the same instant that gratitude wanted to leap from his lips, jealousy took root in his heart.

"Let's go. Reggie is scammered, and I'm getting cold. They're not out here. It's all in your head, Kat," Bella's tone brooked no argument, and the troop headed back inside.

Jonathan rolled on to his back. "I'm sorry."

"No one can apologize for Reggie. That's his expected behavior. Atrocious. Unceremonious. Odious. But unfortunately not shocking."

Somehow Jonathan could still detect a smile in Margaret's tone, "That was exhilarating." She pecked him on the cheek. "Although, I believe we should not test fate for a second time tonight." She leaned over for a second kiss. "Tomorrow!" And then she tiptoed off leaving him lying in the cool grass.

Chapter 12

JONATHAN SAT IN THE cool garden, paintbrush in hand under the observation of Dr. Walker. And the entire time he did so, he couldn't stop thinking about last night. How had Kat noticed their timely departure? What had made her suspicious? If Kat had noticed, who else was as observant? Surely, Margaret and he had been discreet? Well, not entirely, but not much less than perfectly.

If only they had chosen a different location for their tryst, perhaps he wouldn't have been so precariously close to ruining Margaret. And wasn't that where he'd land them if he continued in this vein? He didn't want to ruin her, he didn't want to cause any type of scandal at all. Just being himself in his current condition was cause enough for gossip.

He couldn't figure out what it was about the Colonel that was bothering him. Sure, the Colonel was a handsome man, striking in fact. He was grateful someone had defended Margaret, but was it more than simply being the honorable gentleman? Was the Colonel pining for her? Just biding his time until Margaret noticed him? The

Colonel's words were surely stronger, more personal than the situation necessitated. And he was a whole man, courageous, and of sound mind.

What did Jonathan have to show for himself? Three whole years worth of memories.

Dr. Walker came up and stood behind Jonathan. "Ah, the ever imaginative white sky, I see." He pointed to Jonathan's blank canvas. "Must be my presence making you overthink then, is it?"

Jonathan looked up at the most familiar face he knew. "I wish I had a better answer..."

Dr. Walker slapped him on the back. "Perhaps I'll take a walk around the gardens and then observe any progress on my return."

And off he trotted down the gravel path.

With the mesmerizing crunching sounds of gravel, Jonathan dipped his paintbrush in some shades of pine mixed with basil and started slashing them on the hollow white staring back at him.

MARGARET WATCHED AS JONATHAN finally added paint to his canvas. She breathed in the delight of him perhaps having another breakthrough.

As she continued sweeping clouds in the background, she marveled at the beauty around her. What was left in the autumn blooms, hanging on to the season's last vestiges of warmth, holding out to display their petals for as long as they could. Surely they didn't know of the sleep that awaited them. But she could always rely on them to blossom again in the spring, as if their sleep unknowingly restored them.

Margaret heard Dr. Walker's footsteps crunching toward them, so she rose to stretch her legs and take a gander at Jonathan's painting.

When she caught sight of the painting, her fingers flew loosely to her mouth. There were several thick long lines of dark green weeds. As would be found in the large pond.

"I have confirmed that I am indeed not your muse, my boy." Dr. Walker chuckled, then pointed to the canvas. "What do we have here?"

"Weeds...Just some silly old weeds."

Not so silly, Margaret thought. Did he remember? If he had, he would have been looking at her differently, she was sure.

She wished she could tell him the memory. She wished she could transfer all of her memories into him so he could recall what they shared too many summers ago. But then again, she was also glad she couldn't. The doctor had explicitly said not to share anything more that might disturb or upset him too much. For Jonathan to learn of his family's passing was enough for him to process.

Besides, she and Jonathan had been given a new start together. Feeling this way about Jonathan for a second time was almost too much to bear. Would he prize her as his number one this time? Or would he leave again? The weight was almost too heavy, but she knew her soul wouldn't accept any excuses to carry the load, no matter the poundage. There was no other course of action except to follow her passion for this man who called to everything in her with everything in him.

But at just this moment, a footman came bearing a message for Margaret calling her in another direction. It was requesting her presence for tea with her mother in the pink salon.

Thinking of only the imminent conversation that awaited her, she said the most normal thing she could think of, "I like your weeds." Then she held up the message for Jonathan and the doctor to notice, "I must chat with mother."

And she twirled toward the house and pattered off.

Margaret stood behind the door to the pink salon, calming her breaths. It would do her no good to appear breathless, nor would it be helpful to be distracted. Her mother could read body language like Margaret could read a book, so she wanted her wits about her.

"Hello, dear." Her mother beckoned. "I'm so glad you were free to take tea together."

"Why yes, of course mother."

"It's been too long since we chatted."

Margaret looked at her mother.

"Just the two of us."

Margaret nodded. It had been a while, especially since they had been in such close kahoots in bringing Mary and Gregory together. It did seem as though they hadn't had time together recently.

"Come sit, dear." Her mother patted the settee beside her. "Stay a while." The attempt at levity caused Margaret to give a half smile.

"Thank you. I will." Margaret took her seat beside her mother and noticed the bright dahlias spotting her needlework. "My, you're ever so talented at that."

"Two parts talents, four parts time and effort." Her mother smiled up at her. "Just like you and your artwork. And your abilities on the pianoforte, I might add."

Margaret's cheeks heated slightly at the praise, "Yes, well, you did provide the best tutors." She took a sip of her tea and nibbled on a biscuit.

"Only the best for you and Gregory." Her mother's eyes beamed with pride. "Now tell me what's going on with you and Jonathan?"

Margaret sputtered cookie crumbs. Her mother was rarely this direct. "Jonathan and I?" Margaret scanned her recent memories. Had her mother seen them kiss? Heard them giggling? *Them* giggling? Alright, it would have only been Margaret giggling. Regardless, what was her mother asking right now? Had Margaret given something away? As calm as her mother always was, she knew that in the back of her mind her mother wanted her married.

"Yes. You have been showing him around the estates, have you not? How's the boy's memory coming along?" She was explicitly asking about memories, yet there was an unmistakable twinkle in her eyes. And an unexpected tone coming from her mother. Not chiding. Not praising. Teasing. It was subtle, but it was there. And she had referred to Jonathan as the boy. The boy. She supposed that would be how her mother viewed Jonathan, what with him practically living at their house and being an inseparable part of the foursome growing up together.

With all the possible answers Margaret could give, she chose the most significant, "He's not a boy anymore."

Her mother looked amused. "Yes, I had noticed. I'm not surprised to hear you're conscious of the fact as well. How is our boy? And by that I mean, man?"

Our boy. He is not our boy. He is my boy. I mean, man. He's my man. My man?

Margaret shook her head and wrung her hands in her lap. Then she began tapping her foot.

"What's the matter, dear?"

Margaret could only stare at her mother feeling like a girl caught with a stolen dessert. She was not ready to disclose this newfound revelation of possession. She was hardly ready to accept it for herself. She certainly did not want to divulge any of her feelings at the moment.

"Nothing."

"Nothing?" For the moment, the needlework and tea remained untouched. Her mother keenly observed her and waited. Margaret counted almost eight seconds before her mother continued. "How is he feeling? How are you feeling?"

Margaret took a sip of tea. "Fine."

"Fine?" Eight more seconds passed.

"Well, I'm glad everyone is fine." Her mother picked up her needlework. "That is perfectly...fine."

If only Margaret had known how not fine her mother perceived all things to be, she might have spoken up a bit more.

***

The next day the entire house was awoken to trumpets. Where they came from, Margaret had no clue. But she discovered soon enough that her mother had some surprising plans for the house party this week.

"Thank you all for gathering in the drawing room. And so promptly." The dowager duchess skimmed the room, nodding to the various clumps of haphazardly dressed guests. "I know this is entirely unusual, but I was hoping to inspire you all with a game this morning. Winter will soon be here, and we must take advantage of every nice day before that time arrives. I have been planning a surprise for you all, and I'm entirely delighted to say that the weather has cooperated enough to indulge us. Therefore, today we are going to have a lawn game tournament."

A few gasps with a smattering of clapping echoed in the room. Then without missing a beat, a few murmurs inquiring of breakfast flitted around.

"Breakfast will be served shortly, and picnic baskets will also be provided to each pair as you compete in the games."

Margaret made eyes with Jonathan anticipating their partnership.

"I have the ladies' names in one basket and the mens in another. I'll draw for teams."

Within a few moments, Margaret realized this was not going to be the morning of amusement and merriment she had expected.

Agatha was paired with Reggie. Kat was paired with Lyle. Charlotte was paired with Davin, Viscount Ingleby. Margaret was paired with Colonel Hastford, and Jonathan was with Bella.

Before she could even think of implying a swap, her mother decreed, "No changing partners. Now, let's begin."

Apparently the trumpet had come from the Earl of Winchester and he was beyond ecstatic to blow the horn for each new game. And each round of each game. That is, until he grew fatigued and spent the rest of the morning under the canopy sitting in one of the cushioned armchairs eating tarts the footmen had arranged.

The first game was horseshoes. Margaret clapped her hands then grabbed Colonel Hastford's arm. She let out a short squeal. "We'll surely win this one. I've perfected the toss."

The Colonel's grin split his face. "Then I believe we are off to an excellent start in this competition."

Margaret couldn't be sure, but she thought she heard Jonathan scowl at her. Yes, now she was certain she had heard the scowl.

And then, "Bella, how would you rate your tossing abilities? Nil, fair, outstanding?"

"I daresay it would be untruthfully humble to say nil, or fair, but I cannot bring myself to claim outstanding."

Jonathan chuckled. "Then let your toss do the claiming for you. Come." Walking past Margaret, straight to the game, he handed Bella the first horseshoe.

Bella flipped the shoe softly in the air to catch in her hand, familiarizing herself with the weight. She drew her arm back, then pushed forward letting the horseshoe float in a perfect arch. It clanged around the stake in the ground.

As Bella turned toward Jonathan, Margaret noticed that she had the audacity to blush. Blush! Bella never blushed. This did not bode well for the game.

When it was Margaret's turn to toss the horseshoe, she couldn't remove Bella's blushing face from her mind, and instead of floating the horseshoe around the stake, she flung it wide.

"Perfection is in the eye of the beholder," Jonathan commentated.

"Oh hush," Margaret unsuccessfully feigned nonchalance.

The rounds continued until it was only Jonathan and Bella competing against Margaret and the Colonel. The other pairs had drifted off for early snacks and refreshments.

It was down to one toss: Margaret. If she made it, they would win.

Margaret inhaled slowly and then exhaled, counting to ten. She pulled her arm back and then swung it forward. She launched the horseshoe–

Bwa! The tantara of the trumpet sounded. "Tea time!" Her mother's voice called out.

The horseshoe landed wide.

"We won!" Bella exclaimed. Jonathan grabbed her hands, and they did a silly jig together, then folded over in laughter.

How utterly inappropriate, Margaret scowled as loud as she could.

The Colonel ducked his head beside her ear, "If the trumpet hadn't blasted at that exact moment, I have no doubt in my mind we would have won."

"Mmhmmm," Margaret hummed her agreement. She should have been placated at his reassuring words. At the very least. Then when he took her arm in his and led her to the picnic baskets, she should have been distracted by him and his good nature.

But she was only distracted by the godawful, two-timing, jig-dancing nature of the dolt behind her.

Chapter 13

J ONATHAN WATCHED MARGARET CHOMP each bite of
fruit into her mouth. Her jaw was set, he wasn't sure how she was
even chewing, and she had a flare in her eyes.

The troops were sitting under the canopy on cushions eating a
nice picnic of cold meats, biscuits, and raspberry cake. There was
lemonade and tea served, and each person had helped themselves to
a few servings.

Before everyone else had finished their current refreshments, Margaret had popped to her feet and was urging the Colonel to do the
same.

"Off we go! To a game of shooting now," Margaret declared. She
pointed her finger in the air and whirled it around conveying some
coded message to the troops still lazing about under the canopy.

Jonathan lip twitched into a half smile as he watched Margaret
march off toward the targets.

"I don't think I've ever shot a gun before," he overheard Agatha confide in Reggie.

"Don't worry, pet, I've shot enough for both of us," Reggie reassured her.

"Well, that's just fine then."

"We can't let those two sneak in any practice shots," Kat said loudly enough to Lyle for the group to hear.

That stoked a fire under a few bottoms, and soon everyone was tromping off down the lawn not wanting to be left behind and miss out.

Jonathan turned toward Bella, still sitting in her chair sipping tea. He reached for her hand, "Lady Bella?"

"Why thank you." She stood and smoothed her skirts. As she took his arm, she said, "I should warn you, I'm a terrible shot."

Jonathan scoffed, "I'm sure you're not that bad."

But she was. Almost worse than he had predicted Agatha would be. The ladies' shots were flying wide, even after some pointers. Only Margaret's were consistently hitting the target. Jonathan had been dead center every shot and was the only reason he and Bella were still in the standings.

"I can't seem to make this part–"

"Whoa!" Reggie screeched as he saw Agatha waving the gun around in the air. "Alright, little thing, that's enough guns for you today." He disarmed Agatha and put the gun on a nearby table.

Kat declared, "You two are disqualified."

"But–"

"Safety first." Kat nodded her head. "Now I believe it's my turn. She took aim and shot high. Into the branches. Something fell out of the tree.

"Eek!" Kat shrieked. "Was that a...?"

"Oh dear! The feathers!" Agatha choked up.

"Was it?" the ever stoic Kat looked as though her eyes were turning bleary.

"What are the chances you hit a bird?" Egged Reggie. "What a shot!"

"It wasn't a bird. Just a branch. Nothing to fret about," Lyle patted her arm. Despite her best efforts to hide it, Kat was shaken.

"I think I need some lemonade," she said to no one in particular. When her request went unanswered, she repeated it. "Lyle?" She raised her eyebrows at him and swept her arm out to the side in order for him to steady her and escort her to a safer, quieter, less explosive place.

"Looks like we're out," Lyle ceded.

"You didn't stand a chance, y'foozler," Jonathan taunted.

"That reminds me. About our chess matches–"

"Where's Davin?" Jonathan interrupted with a grin.

The groups stood looking around, counting the numbers, peering toward the bushes. "Has the old gibface fallen asleep? He's been known to do that," Reggie uttered unhelpfully.

"I believe..." Charlotte's cheeks turned a light shade of pink. "He's temporarily detained. At the moment..." It was not ladylike to mention such things as chamberpots or body functions, and of all the ladies to feel the embarrassment, not only to have to hold secret knowledge, but also to have to allude to it, Charlotte was the obvious choice for fate.

Saving her from turning any darker shades of pink, Jonathan said, "Alright, looks like it's just me and the Colonel."

"And me," Margaret chimed in.

"You have no shots left. It's just me and the Colonel." Jonathan turned toward the Colonel. "What say you? Who will shoot first?"

"I believe it's your turn," the Colonel said.

Jonathan loaded his gun, took aim, and shot.

Bang! Nearly dead center. It was one of the best shots of the afternoon.

"Nice shot," the Colonel lauded. "But perhaps," he said as he loaded the gun. "Not quite as nice..." he aimed. "As this." BANG!

Jonathan stared at the target. *This wasn't a big deal. There was little to no importance of this event. It did not signify.*

How many more ways could he think it? He was sure it wouldn't help at the moment. Before he could analyze how he was thinking or what he was feeling, he let himself be immersed by his competitive nature, and then he rose up. He puffed out his chest and inhaled heavily.

"Good shot," he eyed the Colonel who was smiling softly at Margaret. "There's only one way to determine the winner. To the horses!"

MARGARET HAD WANTED TO win, so she was delighted when the Colonel hit the bullseye. Wasn't she?

Right after the Colonel shot, Margaret had turned first to Jonathan, and she saw a flicker of something in his eyes. She couldn't label it, for she didn't have time. And it was gone before anyone else could assess the look, so she couldn't interpret it with Bella. Not that she wanted to discuss such peculiarities with Bella right now. How could she stand there with Jonathan and compete with him knowing what Jonathan meant to Margaret? It was reprehensible. And Jonathan was in on it.

She pushed away her thoughts as the troops walked toward where the stablehand had prepared two horses.

"Where are the rest of the horses?" Margaret inquired with as much calm as she could muster.

"Her Grace said to prepare two horses," Henry, the stablehand, answered.

"So what will the Colonel do as I race against Jonathan?" She hadn't noticed the lack of a side saddle.

Henry fiddled with a button on his shirt.

"I'm racing against the Colonel," Jonathan spoke up.

"But–"

"Apparently there are no buts. Your mother has arranged the day."

Margaret harrumphed in a most unladylike fashion. "I can't believe–"

"Take it up with her."

"I've been competing just as much as–"

Jonathan waved to the canopy.

The dowager duchess was about fifty paces away but somehow saw the motion and acknowledged the wave with one of her own.

If Margaret hadn't been in possession of more self-control, she would have surely been mumbling to herself about how ridiculous this all was. In fact, she wasn't sure she hadn't been grumbling aloud, since Reggie was giving her quite an odd look.

A few footmen directed the guests to watch the race while the riders prepared themselves. Despite not being on the horse, Margaret could feel the pounding in her chest. She wanted to win. Not just for the sake of winning, though that would be a reward in and of itself. She wanted to prove herself. It all sounded silly in her head now. What was she trying to prove? And to whom?

Then there was a loud crack and the horses were thundering down the field. Margaret could feel a bead of sweat forming on her brow, and she whisked it away.

Aloud, she began cheering for the Colonel. "Come on! You can do it, Colonel!" But the second the words were out of her mouth, she realized that for her lips to form the Colonel's title was the most difficult task of the tournament so far.

She cheered again anyway. And then mid-shout she realized that although her voice said *Colonel*, her heart was rooting for Jonathan.

Margaret focused her attention back on the race. Jonathan was two strides behind the Colonel. *Come on, Jonathan. Just three more... You're almost there.*

And then he was. She watched his powerful legs command the horse to do the impossible. Fly. Jonathan and his mount gained on the Colonel and overtook him by a few extra paces.

Margaret's heart was singing. She almost felt teary eyed as she watched the riders dismount. There was no reason for it. Jonathan was a strong, complete person. He didn't need this win for anything. Yet, when Margaret found his eyes, she blinked back a tear.

Bella eyed her curiously.

"The wind," Margaret explained as the trees stood preternaturally still.

JONATHAN TRIED TO DISCREETLY meet Margaret's eyes as he was receiving slaps on the back for his win. It wasn't an important win. There was no significance for it. Yet, Jonathan felt in his core that somehow he needed it.

He glanced over at Margaret and saw her wipe at her eyes. He needed to find time alone with her. Scratch that. He needed to make time alone with her. They hadn't seen each other privately since the tryst in the garden, which was hardly long enough to be called a tryst.

"Congratulations to us," Bella said to Jonathan. "I believe Her Grace as a small token to bestow on us as a gift."

"What a fine end to the tournament." Jonathan grinned. "And you played an excellent part in our win by the way. So yes, congratulations to us."

Bella smiled and then turned to grab Agatha's arm to walk together back to the canopy.

Margaret was being waylaid by the Colonel. Was he milking his loss? Maybe Jonathan should have lost on purpose? What the devil was he thinking? There was no rational explanation for someone to lose on purpose.

"Colonel," Lyle shouted. "I didn't get a chance to ask. Tell me what it takes to become a good marksman."

"You'll never believe me if I told you."

"What's that?"

"Shooting."

The two barked a laugh as they headed toward the house.

Jonathan and Margaret had now serendipitously become the stragglers.

"Quite the ride, wasn't it?"

"It wouldn't have been, if it was me you were racing against."

Jonathan chuckled. "That much I'm sure is true." He stared down at her delicious red lips and recalled her peach taste and jasmine scent. He had ridden that horse for himself. He had wanted to beat the Colonel. He had ridden that horse to win. But a small part of him latched on to the idea that he had been riding for Margaret.

What was it about her? She was unlike any woman he had known before. Well, he supposed that wasn't saying much at the moment. But he had eyes for no one except her. Was that enough though?

"We need to talk, Margaret."

"So serious, Jonathan?" Her lashes fluttered as she peeked up at him. "You've been playful with Bella all day, and now you're all serious with me." She crossed her arms and let out a puff of air.

He stalked over to her and now stood only a few inches from her. "Do you want me to treat you the way I treat every other girl?"

She had to lift her head to meet his eyes, and it stole his breath.

"I want you to treat me like I'm the only girl."

And then before he could think of a reply, she spun around and skipped off.

Chapter 14

MARGARET SAT GRUMPILY AT the breakfast table the next morning with jammy fingers, as she placed another bite into her mouth. She was early enough that she hoped to both catch Jonathan and beat those who slept in. Which shouldn't be too difficult since many of the guests had mentioned plans to sleep until noon.

Jonathan, expectedly the only other person in the room, had just piled some eggs and toast onto his plate and was about to take his seat, when Margaret couldn't hold it in any longer. She knew she was about to pick a fight, but truth be told, the fight was inevitable. The question was of whether she had the fight internally, giving him no chance for input, or externally, where the man might at least get a word in. Probably.

Ding. Ding. The fight bells rang in Margaret's head.

"How are you feeling about yesterday?" Margaret asked sweetly.

"Fine."

That was the word. He got one word in, and a devil of a word it was. *Fine? He was fine?* He wasn't feeling any of the turmoil Margaret was feeling? She could hardly stand to see Bella, one of her dearest cousins, clinging to him all day. There was no time to analyze the exaggeration. Objectivity was beyond Margaret's current capabilities. At least, her current willpower.

She wanted to know how Jonathan was feeling and where his head was at, but she knew how strong she could come on at times. She certainly didn't want to frighten him away permanently, but at the same time...she needed to know.

Margaret finally pulled her gaze back to Jonathan. "Fine?"

Jonathan cocked his head to the side, but before he could get his second—or more—word in, a footman entered the breakfast room delivering a message.

"Your Grace," the liveried footman bowed as he proffered the tray to Jonathan.

The tray glimmered in the morning sunlight as Jonathan took the letter in hand and began reading. Margaret watched his eyes scan the note. They turned dark as his brows drew together.

"I must go," Jonathan rubbed his hands up his face, then stood abruptly looking side to side. "I'm sorry, Margaret. But I must go." With that, Margaret could only watch him march off out of the room.

JONATHAN COULDN'T BELIEVE THE timing of the letter he had just received. He had been waiting for any news on himself and his past, and just when the situation with Margaret was growing...complicated...it grew even more so.

The letter was from one of Gregory's solicitors in London. They said they had news about Jonathan and how he ended up in Glaston. They had requested Jonathan to visit London for more information at his earliest convenience, but in his mind there was no earlier convenience than now. His hosts would understand.

He changed his clothes to better endure a long ride, donned his hat, and left.

When at last he arrived in London, he made all haste to go directly to the office of one Mr. Swanson, in the employ of Gregory, Duke of Wellingford. Such prodigious titles. Perhaps soon Mr. Swanson would be employed by Jonathan as well. Such trivial thoughts ran through Jonathan's mind to distract him from his real concerns. *What had they found? Why now? Would it help to know?*

Jonathan burst through the doors and immediately caught sight of Mr. Swanson's assistant.

Jonathan started to announce himself. "Duke of–"

"Right this way, Your Grace," the assistant had likely been the one to relay the message from Mr. Swanson to the messenger, so was not more than a tad nonplussed to recognize that this was Jonathan when he practically barged in the office.

He led Jonathan into an elegant office of charcoals and creams, seating him in a cushioned chair after he made the introductions.

"Your Grace," Mr. Swanson began.

"Jonathan, please."

"Jonathan then, I'm not surprised to see you hear so soon. I had imagined you would end the dolorous wait with expediency."

"Post haste indeed."

"Your timing is impeccable. Jake Edgely, the bow street runner investigating this for us had planned to meet for lunch to review his final comments." Mr. Swanson checked his timepiece and tapped it twice. "He should be here shortly."

"That is—" the assistant's knock interrupted his reply.

"Mr. Edgely, sir."

"Send him in," Mr Swanson declared.

"Sure glad I had planned to come back to see you today, Mr. Swanson." Jack Edgely looked over to Jonathan and slowly let out a whistle.

"Well, I'll be. Nice to finally see the face I've been investigating." Jake ostensibly recognized Jonathan from the miniature Gregory provided them.

"I guess you're here to hear all about it now, aren't you?"

Jonathan stood perfectly still. He thought he would have been shaking the information out of the man, but now in this brief moment before past met present, he wanted to wait, dwell, and absorb everything he possibly could.

Why had he left Margaret so quickly? Why hadn't he given an explanation? He hadn't decided about whether he wanted her to know yet or not. How would he manage the truth? It was enough to think about, nevermind managing her anticipation and reaction to everything. He had planned to disclose everything to her in time. Once he knew. And once he knew what to do about it. But this morning, and right now, he had no clue what he was going to hear or how he would react to it.

"Glad we're sitting for this one," Jake broke into his silence. "Where should I start?" It wasn't a question, just a musing. And then Jake proceeded to divulge the truth.

"It started with Gregory asking us to find out what happened. A few years ago when you first went missing that is." He paused to scratch his head, "Couldn't find out nothing. For years."

Jonathan's eyes must have widened because Jake filled in, "He didn't tell you we looked that long? Well we did. Longer than he'll admit to you. Anyways, then you returned and Gregory threw more money at it." He clucked his tongue. "This time we had a starting place, Glaston." He rubbed a hand down his thigh. "Thank God for Glaston." He murmured.

"I couldn't agree more."

"Of course the doctor knew nothing, but he was a good fellow. He gave a description of the sailor that brought you to him and the boat you had been on. I guess he had you detained in the hospital for a while so you couldn't do your own investigating."

Jonathan nodded. It had taken some physical restraints and then a hell of a lot of persuading to convince Jonathan that he didn't have the resources, and health, to rely on to conduct his own investigations. The doctor kept saying he might wake up one day and remember everything. One day turned into two. Two turned into ten, and then instead of days, months went by. And Jonathan had been content with the doctor. He had regained his full strength over several months and wherever there were gaps in the skills expected of Jonathan, Dr. Walker had been quick and more than happy to educate or train him.

"No matter. I can't say how much you would have uncovered on your own, especially without the funds I had access to."

Mr. Swanson glared at Jake. "Ah well! Someone should tell the man what a loyal friend he has.

Jonathan was speechless. He knew Gregory was his best friend, but he had had no indication of the time and money spent by him.

"Anyways, back to the story. I followed the trail as far as I could, and then looped back around it several more times. The sailor and captain who dropped you at Glaston didn't know how you lost your memory or who you were. It seems as though you slipped onto the boat under an assumed identity. I spoke to each person who boarded the ship and finally tripped on some gossip. Thank God for husband-hunting mothers. She remembered a dashing but brooding man whom she had hopes of introducing to her daughter. Turns out that man had also used an assumed identity. John Smith. I got an accurate description of the man and just a few weeks ago found him dead. I saw the body, so I'll spare you the details."

Jonathan winced but then nodded for Jake to continue.

"We didn't reach out to you right away because there was more to the story. I pounded on the doors of the war office again. Of course they were tightlipped and revealed nothing." Jake shook his head and clucked his tongue again. "So I had to get crafty. I found the weakest link and began hounding him for information. Finally he delivered. Not much, but I got a working hypothesis on it all now."

Stunned, Jonathan uttered, "That's it? A working hypothesis?"

Jake glared at him, "That's it. It's a working hypothesis because we won't get anyone from the war office formally issuing an apology for sending in an untrained spy to do an impossible task against possibly one of the most lethal agents out there." Jake wasn't finished though, "It's a working hypothesis," he drawled the last two words, "because we can't have a dead man confirm the events."

"There must be a way to confirm it."

"There ain't."

"There must be."

"The only way this'll ever be confirmed is if some guilty conscious pens you a personal note on their deathbed. Too few people know anything at all, and for those that do, there's too much at stake for them."

"What is it then?" Jonathan demanded.

"That's just it. You went ahead on a reconnaissance mission you likely weren't properly trained for. How you were appointed that mission is more than half the mystery. Your direct superior officer was killed, and everyone else knows nothing or one word: mum. The word on the street is that your superior had it out for you, seems like you were engaged to the woman he loved." Jake must have read the frustration in Jonathan's core. "I know it ain't what you want to hear. But it's all you'll ever get."

"Go on."

"You must have followed John Smith onto the boat, trailing him for some information. He grew wise of the fact and knocked you out. Now at this point in the story, three of the sailors can corroborate the fact that you were unconscious because they helped John Smith lug you back to your room."

"Why would they do that?"

"More accurately, they must have caught John Smith about to dispose of you, maybe overboard. John Smith claimed you were drunk, so it's lucky those three came upon you. Otherwise you might be... Well, anyways. They took you back to your room and notified the captain who got involved at that point. He had you monitored since you wouldn't wake up right away. Then when you finally came to, you didn't remember nothing. And the rest, well, at least you know that."

Jonathan sank back into the chair. He had no words. No thoughts. No memories came pouring back. He didn't realize he had been expecting a flood of memories until they didn't come. Then the disappointment of their absence overtook him. He just had nothing. Nothing save a few years of memories and a few weeks of awkward...bliss.

Was it truly blissful? That he could be in the company of a woman who was considered too much while he rightfully would be judged to have too little? Sure, he was a duke. And that in and of itself would get him places, but as a person, he felt as though he didn't have enough to offer anyone. And yet, his time with Margaret was filling. Maybe his time with her was filling the gaps, trickling in to fill places of his heart and mind he hadn't been paying enough attention to the last few years.

Now that he had some answers, certainly not all of them as he still held out hope for more, but at least some, he should be pushing for more information. He should keep digging and not give up the pursuit. Except he had no inclination whatsoever to do that. The only thing he could think of were Margaret's jammy little fingers from this morning, and he wanted to know if it was raspberry or strawberry jam. Then he lambasted himself for how he had left her and not explained anything.

She was going to be furious. He would have his work cut out to change that fury into a fire that burned more pleasingly.

Chapter 15

J ONATHAN FOCUSED HIS MIND on getting back to and making it up to Margaret. How could he have just left her like that? What kind of man would do that?

He would play neither the rake nor the rogue, only himself. If that wasn't enough...well, of course that was his worst fear.

He made one small stop to make before saddling up for the journey back to Chatsworth. *Chatsworth*. Who would have known one word could lead him to such happiness. If nothing else, he thanked his mind for remembering that one word.

On the ride returning to Margaret, Jonathan played the scene over and over again in his mind.

He could find her right away and sweep her off her feet. If she was sitting in the garden, he would march right up to her, whisk her off her feet, and carry her to her room, regardless of witnesses.

He could wait until night to sneak into her room and then show her all the ways he had been dreaming of her.

He could invite her to a game of chess—no definitely not chess. He could invite her to paint with him, just to spend time with her doing what she loved.

Maybe. Maybe. Maybe. All maybes. Until he saw her, he wouldn't know his most advantageous course of action.

By the time Jonathan rode up to the front door, he should have been weary from the trip, but he was a flurry of energy. He reached deep within himself to breathe and calm down. But his legs somehow missed all the signals and they marched into the house in search of Margaret.

Bugsby opened the door in anticipation of the hunt, and as he bowed, said, "Your Grace."

"Where is she?" No explanation necessary.

Delivered without missing a beat, "In the drawing room, Your Grace," Bugsby took Jonathan's topcoat and hat. With the gift wrapped and tucked under his arm, Jonathan strode off toward the room, his heart rate two beats for every step.

He didn't know what he had expected exactly, but he certainly hadn't foreseen every possible guest taking tea with Margaret at the crucial moment when he needed to talk to her.

Now, he could have cleared the room. Or even taken Margaret aside. Had he known the mess he could avoid, he would have. But not being a seer, Jonathan stuck to his gut, which was telling him to wait for his opportunity with Margaret.

"Your Grace," several voices chorused in greeting.

Jonathan nodded absently at all the houseguests still in the dwelling. He took a seat close to Margaret and instructed his hands to take a cup of tea.

"How was your trip to London?" Lyle got straight to the point.

Jonathan quirked a brow.

"It's no secret in a house this small and a situation as large as yours. Come on. We needed something to talk about all day," Lyle offered a sly grin at him.

"Well, if you must know, it was quite productive."

A few heads discreetly tilted his way. Margaret eyed him curiously. The depth of her eyes was inaccessible and all he could read from them was apprehension.

He keenly caught her gaze as if to check in with her. He received nothing back in reply. He needed to elicit some kind of reaction from her, so he spoke. "I may as well tell you what happened." And then he recounted how and what Jake Edgely had uncovered about him.

When he announced the death of John Smith, he heard a few gasps along with a couple of tongues clucking, and by the end of the retelling, all eyes and ears were indiscreetly turned in his direction.

Everyone's except Margaret's. She had found something particularly interesting in her tea, perhaps she was taking up tea leaf reading.

Why was she so aloof? He had just provided one of the most interesting tales anyone in that room had likely ever heard—especially given it was all truth and not tale at all.

"Now what?" Lyle prompted Jonathan.

"Now...nothing."

'At least you know."

"Yes, there's that." Jonathan tried to catch Margaret's eye again, to no avail.

"Do you wish there were more?"

"I do. But I shall come to accept what I know. Meanwhile, I shall continue to hope for the return of my memories.

"That's quite the story you have there," Lyle whistled nonplussed.

"Stranger even than some plays I've attended at your very own Vauxhall, Mr. Fairfax," Colonel Hastford added.

"That awful John Smith," Kat clucked. Jonathan could now identify where at least one of the clucks originated. "At least he got what he deserves."

"Katherine," her mother, the Countess of Winchester, chided quietly.

Kat sipped her tea. Defiantly. It would do no good to rebut in public. Agatha sat mesmerized by her tea leaves in a similar fashion to Margaret, and the gentlemen took turns flitting glances about the room.

During the short distraction, Jonathan leaned toward Margaret and mouthed the words "present" and "for you" to Margaret.

She turned her head back to her tea leaves. Hopefully she was foreseeing a fast-approaching reunion between the two of them.

Jonathan fielded a few more queries from Davin and Lyle before the conversation turned to the topic of winter and the impending weather change.

MARGARET WAS SEETHING TO the point she thought if Jonathan were any closer he would be indelibly burned from the rage emanating from her body. This man. The one she had fallen for before. Lost. Waited for. Cried over. And now was falling for again, had no concept of the repercussions of his actions.

She had to leave the room before she exploded. "Tea was lovely," she nodded to her mother and curtsied to the room. "I think I shall go for a walk before dinner this evening."

The dowager duchess flicked her a look, but responded, "Yes, dear."

Margaret had just passed through the door when she thought she heard her mother say something about bringing a coat.

Forget that. Margaret's fury was all the warmth she needed.

Just as she was about to step outside, she heard the familiar gait of Jonathan. Grumbling, she said, "What are you doing?"

"I came to walk with you," he grinned unknowingly. "And offer my coat in case you grew cold."

"I don't need it. I'm perfectly warm enough, thank you."

Jonathan held out his arm for her to take.

"And I don't need that either," she said.

"Mar–"

"Just leave me alone." She turned around and took off to her room. She heard Jonathan's steps close behind her.

She knew she hadn't stood a chance of outrunning him, so when she reached her room, she resigned herself to leaving the door open. As she waited for him to enter, she took inventory of anything she might possibly want to throw against the wall if the argument erupted. There was a small brush. A handheld mirror. A pitcher. Not much. But it would make a loud enough crash.

"What do you want?" She glared at him. "You shouldn't be here."

"You can't have it both ways," he teased.

She narrowed her eyes to barely opened slits.

"I can either answer your question and stay, or leave and deprive you of the knowledge you seek."

"I don't care." She folded her arms.

"I think you do."

"I don't care what you think."

"I think you do."

The argument, if one could call it that, was already running in circles.

"Argh! You don't know what I want."

"So tell me."

He made it sound so simple. What did she want? Just tell him. If only it were that simple. Since he had arrived at Chatsworth claiming he remembered only its name, nothing had been simple. Did she want him to remember everything? Anything? Which would be easier? There was no easy or simple in this scenario. There was too much old pain to relive and too much future pain potentially awaiting her.

With three words, he could almost reduce everything to a simple transaction. *Tell me what you want. And I'll give it to you.* The second part was implied. That had always been Jonathan's charm. Light. Breezy. Carefree.

When he had returned, she saw him anew. He was anything but breezy. He was made with a hard exterior that no breeze could penetrate. Yet, after spending more time with him, she felt as though some of her breeze was finally filtering through to him. Was it possible? Was it just her imagination? Because then these last two days happened and she questioned everything even more.

While she was ruminating, Jonathan had stepped closer to her. "Tell me, Margaret." His melodic baritone sang to her heart.

"Alright. Let's start with yesterday. What were you doing with Bella?"

"Bella?" Jonathan asked with notable shock.

"Yes, Bella. I saw you flirting with her—"

"You mean, competing in the tournament together?"

"I saw you two. I was there. The dancing, the–"

"The horseshoes and shooting," he interrupted.

"And all the rest," she waved her arms around as if that random gesture could convey all the teasing she had witnessed and all the jealousy–yes jealousy, she could admit it now–that she felt.

Jonathan pulled back. "Your mother put us together. Take it up with her."

She wanted to growl at him. She was taking it up with exactly the person she wanted to. "You still had choices."

He paused. A wise move by a wise man if Margaret had been able to admit it. She wasn't able to do so.

"Tell me what's really bothering you."

"That is what's bothering me. And then you went to London and didn't tell me anything. You don't owe me anything, but I thought..."

"I should have told you."

"Yes," his concession was reducing her momentum, but she was still fired up. "And then when you came back, you didn't even tell me everything."

"I told you everything in the drawing room."

"Yes, you told everyone, Jonathan. But what about me?" She knew she was beginning to sound whiny. She knew she shouldn't have any of these expectations on him. She knew he was a free man. A single man. She knew he was her man. She knew she loved him. Again.

"Oh my god, Jonathan." She cried out in anger. She couldn't tell him she loved him. Not now. Not while they were fighting. Not while he still wasn't treating her as if she were the star of his world and the wind in his soul. Not now. She just...couldn't.

"Come here, darling."

"I don't want to." She almost stamped her foot.

"I know, but come here anyways."

She slowly shuffled toward him as he made a stride to fully close the distance.

He put his arms around her waist and she rested her head reluctantly, but comfortably, against his chest.

"I should have told you first. I wanted to tell you. I just hadn't decided when to do so. Forgive me."

No excuses. Just a simple apology. Could it really be this easy between them? Sometimes there were lines in life that once crossed couldn't be uncrossed. She had already walked this line with Jonathan. Could she do it again?

"Here's the thing darling. I learned a great deal in London. But in particular I realized one important fact. You're too much for me." She began to push away from him, but he held her tight. "That's not the best part yet. The thing is, I've got nothing."

She struggled again.

"Margaret, don't you see? You're too much, I'm not enough. Let's just meet in the middle darling."

Chapter 16

H E WAS STILL TALKING but she wasn't hearing a thing because all she was thinking about was whether that was the best line or the worst line she had ever heard.

Then she looked up and found Jonathan staring at her as if he could read her eyes. "It doesn't matter," Jonathan said.

"What doesn't matter?"

"Exactly," Jonathan released his hold on her and stepped away to where he had left a package. He picked up the small wrapped box and handed it to her. "This is for you."

"For me?" Apparently her capabilities were limited to mirroring his words at the moment.

He gave her a lopsided grin. "Just open it."

Margaret managed to make her fingers listen to her will, and slowly they peeled back the wrapping.

Her eyes beheld the most intimate gift she'd ever received: a custom set of paints ground and mixed by a colorman, and it included crimson lake and ultramarine. How did he know her so well? She had never even talked about these colors, had she? Had she ever mentioned the singular joy it would be to have colors mixed for her by someone so talented? She was sure she had never told anyone. How did he know? How did this man, who, truly, didn't know her at all except for the last few weeks, actually know her? He had no working memories of them from before a few weeks ago, yet he could read her and know her. Her heart. Her eyes. Her soul.

She felt again some inextricable unexplainable tie to his soul.

She didn't want to disturb the moment, but she needed to express the depths of emotion she felt. Her heart was pounding so loudly she was sure he could hear it, but she couldn't tell him what her heart was saying, she was too scared. There might never be a perfect time. Was this as close to perfect as she would ever get?

She couldn't answer any of her own questions. But she couldn't hold in the one question, the one word, that she had laboriously restrained from leaving her body.

So she whispered, "Johnny?"

JONATHAN STOOD DUMBSTRUCK. THE sound of the name floated on a breeze through his soul. Two syllables was all it took and everything crashed down around him. Or was it more like everything rose up within him? The walls crumbled, the shell was shed. In its place arose hundreds, thousands, millions of minutes of memories. He wanted to clutch them all fearing they would disappear.

Even if there had been time to catch them all, there was no assurance he could keep them, so he resigned himself to watching the memories spring up and out of his mind like fugacious dreams.

He remembered running about his estates with his brother catching bugs, playing swords. He recalled his first time on a horse. Grey. And nearly falling off several times.

He remembered learning to fish at the stream. Putting bait on the hooks, which disgusted girls.

He remembered his mother's laugh. Longed to hear it again.

He remembered Mary and Gregory and the silly plays the four of them used to put on. How he had not thought then that Gregory and Mary were destined for each other bewildered him.

And then he remembered the fight with Gregory and Jonathan walking out the door. He remembered going to war in attempts to convince his fiancee at the time to cry off. He remembered not wanting the marriage of convenience his parents had aligned for him nearly at birth.

He remembered the army and his superior officer convincing him to take on a simple small reconnaissance mission. To help his country.

He remembered the boat and the feeling of pain on his head from being knocked out.

He remembered Glaston and everything. Everything. How could millions of memories flood his body in such a short time? Or maybe he had been standing like a wall in front of Margaret for an hour. That, he didn't remember.

But one more series of memories submersed him. He remembered the summer before he left, the water, and Margaret. And...everything.

He wasn't thinking about why she withheld everything. She had her reasons. The only thing he could think and say was one of the most important words between them.

"Maggie?"

MARGARET FOUND JONATHAN STUDYING her with long, slow breaths. Her brow curled in nerves upon hearing him finally use the nickname he had given her before. Her eyes widened as she saw the depth in his own. He had called her Maggie. He knew. He knew everything. All of his memories were back. As sure as she knew the inordinate cost of ultramarine, she knew Jonathan knew.

And all she could think in that instant was that she couldn't bear to lose this moment. She flung her arms around him and jumped up with her legs around his waist, knowing he would catch her.

He did.

And then she locked all her fears and worries in the corner of her mind. They would be of no help right now.

"Johnny?" she asked with a smothering kiss.

"Maggie," he replied with hot lips and a determined nibble on her bottom lip. How he spoke and nibbled at the same time was not worth the mental quandary. Her breasts were aching to be touched, squeezed, pressed, so she thrust them against his chest.

With a firm grip on her arse, he took them both to her bed. Lying her down softly, he began pulling the pins from her hair and tossing them onto the ground, a minefield for later.

She could feel his arousal jutting into her waist, so she slid herself up to meet his shaft with her folds.

"Take this dress off of me, Johnny," she begged.

He paused. Knowing he understood the request, and knowing he was truly a gentleman, she expected nothing less than his reply, "Are you sure, Maggie?"

"Yes. I can't bear losing–it." She looked away, blinking back tears. Now was not the time. Right here and now was for joy. Pure bliss. Taking what she had been longing for since their first summer tryst. "I have to...have you."

"I have to have you too," Jonathan agreed with a smile. And then he worked fervently on the buttons of her dress, pulling some layers over her head and some layers down off her legs until she was bare before him. She could feel the chill in the air reaching her delicate skin.

She waved her arms at him.

"What does that mean?" he teased, knowing full well she wanted his clothes off.

"Off. Now."

"I never knew you to be so demanding."

"Yes, you did."

"I stand corrected. And never more happily to be so." Slowly he unbuttoned his shirt to torment her and then sifted his shoulders out of it as he dropped it to the ground. When he reached for the buttons on his trousers, Margaret sucked in her breath.

She wanted this. She craved this. But she truly had no idea what to expect. Sure, there had been some gossip and a couple of books, but nothing compared to the real–

When he finally freed himself, he stood erect, in more ways than one. It was so large, and thick. Margaret was both terrified and electrified at what was about to happen. The jolts of lightning fly through her body were verging on impossible to still.

He must have read her eyes again, "Darling–"

She cut in, "Don't say anything, just come do...anything."

Jonathan grinned at her. "Yes, darling."

With that he jumped on the bed. She winced, thinking she was about to be smooshed, but he had reflexes like a cat.

He put two fingers on her lips. "I know you said not to say anything."

Somehow she managed to muffle out, "Stop saying somefing then."

"I must. For your benefit," and she knew with the intense desire in his eyes, she could trust him. "My only desire is to worship you and your body. But I fear that might be accompanied by some pain. I promise I will make this all about you."

"Us," she muffled out the single word.

Jonathan chuckled. "Yes, this is about us, isn't it? In that case, let me introduce myself."

"I believe you already have," Margaret smirked.

"That's enough out of you, my lady," he leaned down and shut her mouth with the most foolproof plan.

Margaret could sense every throbbing point of her body that was in contact with Jonathan. His heat was charging into her and she could feel the ache between her legs growing. It was like nothing she had ever experienced.

Jonathan brushed her hair off her neck to taste more of her skin. He drew his hand down her leg and began to tickle the top of her thighs with small swirls, slowly inching closer and closer to her ache.

Margaret felt him touch her wetness and she moaned, sensing the approaching pleasure. Then he dipped his finger into her folds and she arched into him. She yearned for everything he could give her. "Johnny, I need you."

"Mmm," he soothed her then teased her more, bringing her to the brink of despair.

"Please."

"What do you want?"

"I don't know."

"Where do you want it?"

"Here," she pushed herself into him and he slid his fingers into her. She groaned as he touched her senseless. The wetness seeping between her legs begged for more release.

"I think..." She was sure he had left his sentence intentionally hanging because his grin was too broad to be coincidental.

"What do you think?" she panted.

"Yes, you're ready for me." He nudged his shaft against her entrance and slid into her in one smooth motion. There was no pain, only...some discomfort, then oh, glorious pleasure. Like nothing she could have ever imagined.

"Johnny!"

"Yes," he moaned. She could see him slowly losing his grasp on reality. He had one fist clenching the sheets and the other gripping her hip. A low growl came from the back of his throat.

"I need you."

"I need *you*," the words escaped in a grunt as he thrust in and pulled out. She was bereft until he plunged into her again.

"Oh!"

"That's it, darling. My darling, Maggie."

And then all sense and thought left her body for the briefest instance, as if to collect every possible ounce of sense and thought in the entire universe, only to come bounding back to her and completely saturate her.

Her insides convulsed around Jonathan. Mouth open, her name was a growl, ferocious, protective, insane. Then he leaned forward and collapsed on top of her.

Still inside her, he kissed her shoulder, her neck, her face. He shuddered and then withdrew, and a part of her she had never acknowledged was missing.

"I never knew it would be like that, Johnny," she said almost demurely.

"I never knew it could be like that, Maggie," he kissed her arm and rolled to his side. "That was the most singular, most amazing experience of my life."

Margaret propped herself up on her elbow and swatted him, "Oh don't say that."

"It's true!"

"But you have had–"

He grabbed her in his arms and rolled them both over until he was hovering over her, "Maggie, I'm telling you. It has never been like that before. This. It was like it was my first time. You. You are my first. You are incredible."

She beamed up at him and saw his eyes reflecting the same joy she felt.

"I told you, you're too much." She swatted him again as he laughed into her neck. "Too much, but I want more." The devilish grin he gave her stole her breath away.

Chapter 17

THE HEAVINESS OF JONATHAN'S arm and leg draped over Margaret's body juxtaposed the lightness in her heart. Love abounded and it took all of her willpower not to whisper her heart in his ear. She was the impulsive one. It would have been normal for her to shout out something so weighty with a breezy comment.

But for these words, she wanted to pick the perfect time and place to share her heart with him. She could make an argument for this–naked and fully draped with the one she loved–being the perfect time and place, but truth be told, she really wanted to hear it from him first. Was that selfish? Immature? She didn't care. She wanted to hear that he loved her.

With those thoughts, she nudged her nose under his jaw, feeling the slight scrape of stubble against her face.

"Johnny?" she murmured to the half asleep body.

"Mmm," he murmured incoherently.

Reluctantly, Margaret chose to be responsible, "I think you had better leave before someone finds you here."

Jonathan didn't reply.

"Johnny?" with slightly more urgency.

"Maggie," he drawled and pulled her underneath his warm body. "Or should I say Your Grace, my duchess of Somersby."

Margaret playfully smacked his chest. "Do not jest of such cardinal matters."

He grinned, "I'm not joking." He nibbled on her neck, "Of course we'll marry now."

The levity floated off Margaret's face. "What do you mean, 'of course?'"

Jonathan fixated on Margaret's eyes. "Maggie," he paused. "I mean of course we'll marry. I'm not a cad. If I don't marry you, then you'll be ruined."

Margaret could feel her pulse rising. She had been in this position before, with Jonathan potentially ruining her. It hadn't happened the first time, and she sure as hell wasn't about to let it happen now. And to think he was only going to marry her out of responsibility. Honor. Duty. No he hadn't said the words, but the sentiment drenched his alternative choice of words: *of course we'll marry.*

She would not marry for anything less than her ideal life. Not perfect, but pretty damn close. No, she would not marry simply out of honor. Not until she had held fate back for as long as she could. She had an entire season left to find love before the real pressure began. She had began to hope she would find love with Jonathan, but this line of conversation was not proving promising.

"Will I?"

"Won't you?"

"I won't."

"Explain."

"This was a choice. My choice–" she put her finger up to his lips to stop him from interrupting her. "Whatever you may think, I was of perfectly sound mind to choose this...course of action. And I can deal with the consequences."

"But–"

"But what? No one even knows that this has happened. Speaking of such," she pulled the covers away from him, wrapped herself in them, and gently pushed him away. "You really do need to go." And for emphasis, "Now."

He stood to his full height and pushed out his chest. "Maggie, we're getting married."

"Johnny," the patronizing word dripped out of her mouth.

Jonathan was yanking on his breeches. He glared at her. "If you think anything short of us getting married is an option, you're sadly mistaken young lady."

Young lady?! Margaret's pulse soared.

Jonathan continued unaware, "This isn't a discussion."

Margaret was seething now. Through clenched teeth, she pushed out the words, "No. This isn't. Now leave." Margaret's glare was shooting round lead balls, otherwise known as bullets, straight at a very specific target, Jonathan's heart.

Being a moving target, Jonathan deflected the bullets by twisting about and shoving his arms into his sleeves. Then he haphazardly threw on his coat. "I'll be in my room when you come to your senses."

"I'll be here when you find where you lost yours."

Jonathan rubbed his hands up his face. "Maggie..." he began. She could see his clenched fists as his side, and the tightening of his neck muscles and jaw. Then he turned and left.

The second the door clicked, Margaret was on a heap on her bed. Why did she have to be so impulsive? Why couldn't she exert even a smidgen more self-control? And why the devil had Jonathan not said he loved her? Surely he did. Didn't he?

JONATHAN WANTED TO RAGE. Loudly. He wanted to slam the door and curse aloud. Instead he quietly pulled the door closed so as not to draw any attention to her room. And the cursing? Well, the invectives stormed loudly, but all inside Jonathan's mind.

Hell and damnation. What the blazes was the chit trying to do? Ruin herself and reap scandal upon her whole family? Did she have any concept what kind of gossip this would cause if somebody found out? And why the hell didn't she want to marry him?

His memory was back now. He was whole. He had everything to offer her from before and then some.

Jonathan's head ached.

He didn't care how, but he was going to make Margaret marry him.

But, *Ow!* His head was actually throbbing. He put a hand to the side of his head to ease the pain. Then he slumped against the wall and the last thought he had before everything went black was, *Maggie!*

MARGARET WAS FUMING. WHAT the hell was wrong with Jonathan? Now that all of his memories had returned, didn't he realize that they needed to talk and sort through everything that had happened before he went missing. He had left her for another woman...practically. Or for the army, at least. It hardly mattered why he left, he left. And then he hadn't returned for three years. Then out of the blue he knocks on Chatsworth's doors claiming he only remembers the name of the house.

She was such a fool to think she could show him around and not get mixed up in it all. But she had a responsibility to share with him what she knew. At least, all that she knew minus the memories that might upset him. Doctor's orders. Oh if only Gregory and Mary, or even one of the others had been here, it would have eased her burden.

It was a burden she carried well. Well, well enough.

Then Jonathan kept having those weird visions about the pond. Their first...experience together. Chills ran up her spine just thinking about it. She had tried not to walk him down that part of memory lane, so as not to disturb him by its painful ending.

Despite the difficulties it brought, she was glad he was back, if only for the sole purpose of introducing her to the effects painting can have on the mind. Yes, that knowledge would serve her well and carry her along in the hope it could bring to so many others.

But for him to think he could just assume she wanted to marry him... of all the ignorant, high-handed–

"Maggie!"

Was that Jonathan? Margaret threw on her chemise and ran out to the hallway. There, in a heap propped up against the wall was Jonathan. Panic seared her heart. She ran over to him, knees trembling.

"Johnny?"

She patted his cheeks, "Johnny! Wake up!" She was on her knees cradling his head in her lap. "Johnny, no. Wake up. You can't do this to me again." Her tears flooded down her face and mingled into his hair. As she brushed back the locks from his forehead, she soon felt someone gently tugging on her shoulders.

But everything was bleary, and blurry, and blunted. Nothing made any sense. She couldn't see or hear anything. Who was holding her? Why was someone taking Jonathan away? She yanked to be free from the grasp around her shoulders. Then she clawed at the arms tightening around her waist.

"Let me go!" She screamed. Her hair was wildly flying about her face, and soon it was melded to her face, secured by the tears.

Then her body plunged forward one more time to reach for Jonathan, but the arms holding her back were too strong. She crumpled to the ground. Another body dropped beside her, "Hush dear. It's ok. He'll be alright."

The words held the weight of air. Air that wisped past her face offering no relief, only taunting her in its mysterious trail.

Margaret awoke later, her eyes heavy and puffy. She could hardly lift her eyelids to slits to see where she was. She patted beside her and glanced around realizing she was back in her bedchambers. Instantly recalling the scene in the hallway, her throat closed and she fought back a sob.

She heard footsteps and her mother was at her side. "Drink this dear." She held a glass of water to her mouth, and Margaret quickly discovered how parched she was.

"Where's Jonathan?" Her mother tried to hide something, but Margaret caught the flicker in her eyes. "Tell me, mother. I need to know."

"My dear, you must rest. He's," she hesitated every so slightly before the word, "Fine."

"Please mother."

"Dr. Walker has been in to see him a few times. He's observing him. It appears as though... he's had a shock."

"Wha–"

"That's all we know right now. There's nothing more to tell. I've probably said too much. Please, my dear, rest." Knowing Margaret wouldn't dare close her eyes, her mother offered the following promise, "I'll wake you as soon as I hear anything."

To assuage her mother's concern, Margaret closed her eyes. Her feigned sleep turned real, and soon she was in a deep slumber.

The sleep was not restful. The dreams haunted her. She could see Jonathan's silhouette, just a shadow of a man, slowly coming into view and then gone. Each time she reached for him, he drifted further away. When she called to him, it had no effect, as if her voice carried no sound. And then in the instance that Jonathan turned to her, she pushed his hand away forgetting she had intended to grab it. She reached and reached, but it was no longer there. She was calling out, but there was no answer.

'It's alright dear. There is no need for apologies. All is forgiven," she could hear her mother's soothing voice trying to reassure her, but she couldn't wake up. She couldn't move her limbs, and her tongue was incapable of speech.

Finally, in her dream, she grasped Jonathan's hand, and then–

Splash!

Margaret sat upright, spluttering. She wiped the dripping water from her eyes and flung her eyelids open.

"What, pray tell, was that for?"

The unequivocal look of relief in her mother's eyes shook Margaret to her core. "Oh my dear, you were ranting and moaning. You seemed to be in such pain. I just wanted you to wake up."

Leaving the dream completely behind her, Margaret acknowledged the stress prevailing upon her mother, "I'm awake."

She studied her mother. *Was there something more? Jonathan?*

"He's fine, dear."

She must have spoken the name aloud. "Please, do not spare my feelings. I must know if something has happened."

"Dr. Walker just came in a few minutes ago to give a brief update. He said that Jonathan must stay in bed for a couple of days with no visitors. He's not to be disturbed. At all."

"No visitors?"

"None."

"At all?"

"At all."

"What is he going to do for two days by himself?"

"I'm sure Dr. Walker will provide him some company. Now, you get your rest. Remember that tomorrow we still have guests to host for a little while longer."

Margaret lay back in her bed. Yes, she could rest. She could let Jonathan be. It was only two days. She'd be distracted by having guests to entertain. Certainly she would pass some time painting.

There was no need to see Jonathan right away. He was going to be fine. The doctor confirmed it. She had to let him heal. Then in two days she could disrupt the buttons right off of him and tell him she was wrong and that of course she would marry him.

She had spent years without him. What was two days?

Chapter 18

T WO DAYS WAS A whole hell of a lot, was what it was.

Day one was actually hell. She stayed in her room nearly all day, wanting to avoid the guests with a particular penchant for gossip. Unfortunately, as she sat in her room reading and painting, she grew exceedingly irritated by the innumerable steps of the footmen that were going to and fro Jonathan's room.

She couldn't imagine the needs of one man for one day. How many books could he possibly be requesting? Meals? Medicine? She stopped trying to make sense of it halfway through the day and instead focused on her painting.

Both her mother and Bella had knocked on her door to see her, but she had declined the visitors pleading a headache. It wasn't exactly true, but it wasn't precisely untrue either. Her head *was* aching as it tried to process everything.

More than once she wanted to slip out of her bed and see Jonathan, but the doctor had seemed quite stern with his demand for Jonathan's rest. Considering his normal jovial comportment, she decided she would respect his instructions. At least for now.

If she thought day one was hard, day two's first few hours were some of the most excruciating hours of her life to date. She had hoped to breakfast with a few guests, as that idea seemed more diverting than being alone in her room again; however, she hadn't anticipated every single guest of the house to be present quite so early.

It seemed as though no one was attempting to be discreet about their ear for gossip. On second glance, that was *no one* minus Lyle. Margaret noticed he was unusually absent this morning.

"How's the duke doing?" Kat jumped right in and voiced the question on everyone's mind.

"He's doing well. He needs a couple of days of rest is all," Dr. Walker met Kat's eyes and then gave Margaret a reassuring lok.

"Has he been cupped?" Reggie asked.

"Actually, I don't practice bloodletting with my patients. Experience has shown them to grow weaker after such actions."

"You don't believe in it?" Reggie probed.

"Not particularly. As I said, it has usually left them done to a cow's toe," Dr. Walker chuckled, and then proceeded to explain more the medical reasoning behind his opinion. "Specifically..." His voice droned off in answer to Reggie's question.

Margaret overheard Agatha whisper to Bella who was sitting right beside her, "I didn't know cows had toes. I think I need to spend more time in the country."

Bella laughed quietly. "You may enjoy spending more time in the country. I know I do. But you won't learn about cows and their toes. The doctor just means bloodlett patients were usually left fatigued."

Agatha smiled and patted Bella's arm. "Well that makes perfect sense, then. You'll have to tell me more about the country sometime."

"I would love that, above all else." Margaret observed as Bella beamed a smile at Agatha.

As the women resumed eating, Margaret decided she needed to make plans with Bella for the morning to avoid losing her mind while waiting for Jonathan to get better.

"Please, Bella, my dear cousin, tell me that, above all else," she gave Bella a sparkling smile, "that you would love to paint with me in the garden after breakfast."

Bella smirked. "While I can't truly commit to that particular task above all else, since I cannot paint a distinguishable blue sky from green grass, nonetheless, I will join you in the gardens." And then she added, "My dear, *dear* cousin."

Margaret gave an unladylike chortle. What felicity to have a cousin such as Bella.

With breakfast finished, the cousins grabbed a few needed items and then headed to the gardens together.

Margaret asked a footman to carry and set up her easel, and Bella was simply kneeling next to the garden bed needlessly picking at some weeds.

Margaret stared at the white canvas in front of her. She needed to paint. She needed to clear her mind and refresh her thoughts. She needed to not think about one thing, one someone, in particular.

So it was uncommonly irksome when Bella blurted out, "What's going on with you and Jonathan?"

Margaret gaped at her.

"Come on Margaret. You couldn't possibly have thought I wouldn't ask about that. I saw you entangled on the garden grass floor for goodness sake. You are so lucky I was the one who first stumbled across you two. Can you imagine the scandal?"

Slowly, she shook her head. Then nodded. Finally finding her voice, she answered, "Of course I can imagine the scandal." Then she mumbled, "It's all I can think about."

"Just tell me then," Bella insisted.

"What's to tell? You saw it didn't you?"

"Well, there must be more going through your mind." If it had been anyone else, Margaret might not have been so willing to share, but she did want to alleviate the burden that her thoughts had created.

"You know me, of course there's more going through my mind. He wants...he wants to marry me."

Bella stopped picking weeds. "When were you going to tell me?"

"I said no."

"You want me to believe that you said no?" Bella repeated in disbelief.

"Well, yes. Why would I lie about that?"

"Why would you say no that?"

"Because he didn't ask me."

"Wait. I'm confused. Did he ask you to marry him or not?"

"He did. What I mean is, he said he was going to marry me. Wait, before you lunge at me–I can see you getting ready for an attack, Bella–he didn't ask. He just assumed we would get married."

"Why would he assume that?" Bella stared at her as Margaret let the silence ring through the air. "Unless..." And then for only the second time in Margaret's memory, Bella blushed. "You didn't. But we were there... How did you... When would... You didn't! Did you?"

"Not then..." Margaret felt the heat crawling up her face now too. "But then later. We...did."

Margaret watched Bella's brows knit together as she mulled over this news. Then, as only Bella could be so pragmatic, she asked, "So what's the problem?"

"He didn't–"

"I know. He didn't ask. I understand. You view yourself as his equal. You want to have a say in it. Blab blab blab. Great points. I agree. But life isn't always like that, is it? He wants to marry you. And, my dear cousin, if anyone should know, you're not growing any younger. So truly, I think the only question is, do you want to marry him?"

Margaret would have walked away or verbally attacked almost anyone else had they spoken to her this way, only a few could get away with it, and Bella was one of them.

She sat like a stump, just eyeing her canvas. A few minutes must have passed.

"Well?"

"I'm thinking."

Margaret sat and thought for what must have been several more minutes, perhaps even an hour or two because when she looked up, she realized she had painted the profile of Jonathan's face. Behind him was her leg wrapped in weeds in the pond.

Bella now stood beside her. She let out a low whistle. Margaret peered up at her.

"What are you waiting for? Just go to him."

The ever-impulsive Margaret just sat for a full three seconds, maybe only two, and then she stood up so fast she knocked her stool over. She reached up to pat her coiffure into place, then pinched her cheeks. "Yes. Oh my god, you're right. What the devil am I doing?"

Bella chuckled. "I don't know."

"What should I do?"

"I don't know. But you do."

"*I* don't know," Margaret insisted.

"Yes you do." Upon seeing Margaret stick her bottom lip out, Bella asserted, "You will know what to do the second you see him. And I'll..." she waved her arm at the painting. "Don't worry. I'll take care of this. I'll have it draped and placed in your room or something. Just go."

Margaret flashed a glance at the painting, then back at the house, then again at Bella. "Alright. Yes, you're right. I can do this." She twirled around, grabbed her skirts, and then raced off toward the house. After racing about a hundred paces she whirled back around to shout to Bella, "I love you! Thank you!" Then she blew some kisses as Bella laughed.

Margaret braced herself to stop and pull on the handle to open the door when out stepped her mother.

"There you are, my dear."

"Hello, mother. I really must–"

"Just one moment of your time, daughter."

In her urgency, Margaret almost missed the use of and tone on the word daughter.

"I have to–"

"Margaret. We need to talk."

Right now? Margaret wanted to scream. *What the bloody hell? This is my moment. I need to speak with Jonathan. I need to see him. I need to tell him that nothing can keep me from him. I can't lose him again. I just can't.*

Her mother must have seen the strangling emotions racking Margaret's face.

"This isn't like last time, my dear."

Margaret's throat closed. How did her mother know her so well?

"He's not going anywhere."

"How do you know?"

"I know."

"That's not good enough."

"It has to be."

Margaret felt the tears burning her eyes. Compelled to go to him, she physically had to refrain by leaning against the exterior of the house and pressing her hands into the stone wall.

"I've been on your side since the beginning."

"But when he first arrived, he remembered nothing. How did you even know who he was anymore?"

Her mother gave her a disbelieving stare, "Since the first time, my dear."

"Really?"

"Truly." She nodded for emphasis. "And now he's back. He's changed. Let him show you. Let him come to you. He will prove himself beyond any of your doubts and fears. Just...be patient."

"How can I be more patient?"

"I understand it's the last thing you want to do right now. But he needs this time. I've never led you astray, my dear. Trust me."

Battling every impulse in her body, Margaret decided that wild horses were the only thing that could keep her from Jonathan. But she'd have to settle for riding a horse wildly.

The wind whipped Margaret's cheeks as she galloped across the fields. Instincts took her to the only conceivable place. The pond.

She dismounted and let the reins drop under the horse's neck. Scanning the horizon, she inhaled deeply. The air was fresh and a slight chill hung in the breeze. She slipped off her shoes and made her way to sit on the bank.

Dipping her toes into the water sent a rush of ice up her legs, but she welcomed the shock and discomfort.

This was the place it had all sparked into being. Her and Jonathan. The man who had, up until that moment under water, had been her competitor, her cheery-eyed, light-hearted, friend.

Now he was a man who had faced death and an infinite amount of unknowns, yet he could still wear the lopsided grin and spray laughter around like water. The depths he possessed with a carefree outlook on life were unmatched.

Staring out at the pond, she could still feel his face between her thighs. As she remembered the moment he nuzzled her, she felt the heat overtake any chilly vestiges from the water. She pressed her fingers to her bottom lip, imagining his overtaking hers.

And then, as if conjured up by her very thoughts, she saw Jonathan approaching.

Chapter 19

J ONATHAN WAS TAKING WHAT had become a customary
  stroll around the pond when he spotted Margaret. He had still
hoped for a bit of time before he was to speak with her, but maybe
fate was forcing his hand.

When he first noticed her, she had her feet dipped in the water.
But now that she saw him, she drew her knees up to her chest, resting
crossed arms and then her head on top. She seemed unusually calm as
he approached.

He waved from a distance and she wiggled her fingers.

"Hello, Maggie." He lowered himself down beside her and placed
his palm on the ground behind her hip. His body yearned to feel her
warmth and softness.

She still hadn't spoken. He intended to fill the silence, but only got
as far as, "I've got a lot to say."

A few seconds passed before she uttered what she had been deliberating over, "That's expected."

Jonathan noticed a gleam in her eye and a curling of her lip while she still coddled her head in her arms.

She looked so vulnerable and peaceful. He wished he had never hurt her, and in so many ways he couldn't have helped. All he could hope for now was that what he had done would show her the truth. He breathed a deep breath.

"I've been busy this last day and a half."

She nodded.

"Under doctor's orders," he rubbed his face, "I've had a lot of time to think about what I want to say to you."

He could see his words were causing undue alarm. "I just have to start somewhere." He shook his head. "I didn't leave you. Before you say you don't believe me. Just listen first. I remember everything now. At least, from my side of things. Back before I went missing, I left for the army in hopes of making my fiancee at the time cry off from our long term engagement." He heard Margaret suck in her breath, and he shook his head again. "I can't get over the twist of fate that met me. I found out my superior office was actually in love with my now ex-fiancee, who by the way married in my absence. Regardless, his unrequited love for my intended was why he encouraged me and then sent me on that mission." He blew out a loud breath. "If only..."

Margaret slid closer to him and reached for his hand.

"I can't believe I lost all this time with you." He rubbed this thumb over her palm as he stared out over the pond. "But I have to thank this pond." He chuckled. "For so much."

He leaned over and kissed her temple. "It all started here. Somewhere over there, actually." He pointed past her body. Then reaching across her, he forced her to lean back, and she rested her head on his bicep as he ran his hand over her waist and up her ribcage.

"Thank the pond, I found you again. You must know how much you mean to me."

Finally, she spoke. He didn't realize he'd been holding himself back, until she pressed upon him two small words, "Tell me."

"You're everything to me. Your smile. Your joy. The way you think about life and other people. Your passions. Your overreactions. And sometimes underreactions." He gently brushed her cheek. "The relationships you have with people, like your mother, Mary, and Bella. Your brother. Your loyalty inspires me. You are open to people and learning about yourself. How you paint to rest your mind and share your heart."

At that Margaret coughed and let out a small laugh. "About that...I'll have to show you something later."

Jonathan grinned. "I'm sure it'll be amazing."

"And then some," she rested her hand against his chest.

He imagined he could stay here forever with her. They cuddled in comfortable silence for a few minutes. But he also knew he had plans to put into motion. Reluctantly, he pushed his elbow into the ground and pushed himself up until he could stand. He drew her up as well, took a few steps around the pond, and then stopped.

"Right here. This is the spot where it all started."

He watched Maggie take in the scene of the pond, and his body warmed, just knowing how much they shared together.

"Maggie, the past two days have been pure torment. I have wanted to see you more than you'll know. But I needed time. In fact, I recruited Dr. Walker to help buy me some time. After his assessment of me, he concluded that I was fine. He thought I was either dehydrated or that I had just overexerted myself." Jonathan smirked at Margaret, "Probably both...But I told him I needed time and that two days should be enough if I worked quickly."

He watched her brows pull down. "You prescribed two days' rest for yourself?"

"In a manner of speaking. I needed time to..."

Feeling a slight tug away from his hand, but he pulled her close. "I needed time to set something up for you. I know you've never wanted to marry just for the sake of marriage, and you've often searched for something more to bring to the table. I believe you've found it painting and using that to help others. At least, for now?"

He waited for her to nod.

"I bought you a building."

Margaret's jaw hung open. "How big?"

"It's in London." That wasn't the answer to her question, but it was the continued flow of his earlier thoughts. "You can start small. Or big. However you like. You can hire a team or appoint volunteers. You can create that society you mentioned. We can get more solicitors, a team of doctors. Whatever you need. It's your–

She pressed her fingers to his lips.

He gently kissed them and then pulled them away. "I just want you to know that I believe in you. I'll support you in whatever dreams you have. I want you to have all of your dreams fulfilled."

Then he dropped to one knee. "And I hope I'm one of those dreams, Maggie. I love you with the very essence of my being. And I have been doing so for a very long time. Will you marry me?"

MARGARET WATCHED HIM DROP to one knee, and everything stilled. There was no longer time, and perhaps there was no longer space. Her soul, her very existence, was tied to his. United as one. She knew it when she was young and innocent. He was the only one she had ever wanted.

She knew it before, and she knew it now.

He was staring up at her and there were a thousand thoughts flowing through Margaret's mind. She wanted to topple him over and kiss him senseless.

She wanted to upbraid him for leaving her in the dark for two days. Alright, one a half, but that was absolutely too long.

A small part of her wanted to demand more details, but first she had to make one thing clear.

"Thank you for the building." Then she threw her arms around his neck. Somehow in the tumble, she had ended up underneath him.

"Is that a yes?"

"Yes. Yes now. Yes before. Yes always."

Chapter 20

T HE NEXT WEEK FLEW by. It was decided that they would
marry before winter weather prohibited an outdoor wedding.
Jonathan pleaded his case with the Archbishop of Canterbury. Along
with a few supplemental words from Dr. Walker and His Grace the
Duke of Wellingford, Jonathan secured a special license to marry
quickly and in whatever locale they preferred. Which was by the pond
of course.

Food was ordered and brought in immediately because the current
houseguests were invited to stay and join in the celebration.

Although Margaret should have been all-consumed with wedding
plans, she had set aside time to write some correspondence in hopes
of gaining some momentum for her–currently nameless– society that
aimed to help others through painting.

However, the night before the wedding, she was exhausted and
didn't want to discuss another wedding plan or business plan item for,

well forever for wedding stuff, and at least a few weeks for business stuff. She deserved a proper honeymoon, to be sure.

As Margaret sat in front of her mirror, she was brushing one hundred strokes through her hair. Normally it was something that Adeline would do, but Margaret wanted time to think.

She was thinking about her future with Jonathan and the children they would have together. She imagined having a boy that looked just like him and could laugh his way through life. Just like his father. Seeing into the years ahead, she could envision Jonathan teaching their children to fish and ride horses. She, of course, would handle the target practices. Chuckling to herself, Margaret could feel the stress of the week and the nerves of tomorrow turning into giddiness. It was a good time to go to bed now.

Unexpectedly, she heard a knock on her door. It was a familiar tap though.

Smiling, she opened the door a crack, and a hand reached through, grabbing her wrist. He whooshed in the room like a fresh breeze. Clad only in breeches and a loose shirt with open collar, she could see the hair on his chest calling her to run her fingers through it. She didn't refrain.

"Maggie, my love. I couldn't wait."

"Wait until tomorrow, you mean?"

"Until any time past now." He smiled, knowingly. "We must finish what we started in here years ago."

"Finish the right way, you mean?"

"Yes, finish both ways. Agreed."

JONATHAN GRABBED HER WAIST and lifted her into the air where she instinctively pulled her legs up and wrapped them around his core.

"You are the very air that I breathe, Maggie." He whispered under her jaw as he licked down toward her breasts.

Her breaths grew shorter and heavier, and she threw her head back, giving him more access. Doing so pulled their weight in the direction of the bed, so Jonathan took the hint and carried her there where he gently tossed her down.

He pulled his shirt off and undid his breeches, his arousal flinging toward Margaret. She could feel an ache building between her legs. Yearning. Craving release.

"My darling, you are beautiful. Let me see all of you." He reached toward her and slowly pulled her nightgown up over her head. With each inch he pulled off, he closed more and more distance between them until he was straddling her.

Throwing the nightgown onto the floor, he used his now free hands to caress her body. Explore every curve and tease her in every place possible.

He leaned in to kiss her and their tongues clashed fervently as he lapped up her intoxicating flavor. Slowly he reached down and massaged her thighs. Then he slid two fingers between her folds and into her cunny. He caught her moans in his mouth and found a rhythm to tease her.

Soon his fingers were drenched in her wetness, but he pressed on.

"Johnny, please."

He pushed in and pulled out again.

"Johnny, please. I need you."

His only response was more teasing. And then he added his thumb to gently massage her holy nub.

"Oh, God. Johnny. I need...you...now." She was on the verge, so he kept on pressing her until she exploded. He felt a small gush around his fingers and her core clenching him.

She was the most beautiful thing he had ever seen. In all her pleasure and glory. "You need me again, you say?"

He whispered huskily into her ear as he withdrew his fingers and she moaned. "Let me give you what you need. Again."

He gently nudged his arousal against her soaked opening.

"Oh Johnny, please."

He pushed himself an inch inside. When he stopped she let out a long moan, so he pushed in another inch.

"Johnny, now, I need you. Again. Now."

He pushed all the way in, to the hilt and let out a groan. "Maggie, you're so wet, my darling."

Holding nothing back, he thrust into her. They moaned together, her pleading for more, him promising to give it.

He thrust in again, harder, moving her up the bed. And again. And again. He was a man unleashed, fully himself, fully embraced by the woman he loved. He thrust again. And then when he heard her cry out and clench around him, he thrust one more time until he released the energy of life into her.

"God, I love you Johnny."

"I love you too, Maggie."

He lowered himself down onto her, still entrenched in her. This was love. This was remembering everything from the past and looking hopeful to the future. Him and her.

He kissed her cheek and rolled over to the side, unsheathing himself from her.

"You had better go–" Margaret started to say.

"Before someone catches me here?"

"Yes," she swatted his arm.

"And what, make me marry you?" He grinned and rolled on top of her again. "Maybe I'll make you scream so loud that someone does run in here to check on you."

"I want to say yes to the first half of that sentence."

"I'll take it."

"Yes, you will."

And he did. A few more times that night before they got married the next day.

***

MARGARET SAT NEXT TO Jonathan on the bank of the pond reclining against his chest. They were taking a few minutes together after the guests went back into the house for refreshments following the ceremony.

The wedding had happened in the blink of an eye. One moment she was Lady Margaret, and the next she was Her Grace, The Duchess of

Somersby. Oddly, the transition wasn't shocking, it simply felt right. As if she'd been waiting for it her whole life.

She knew, without doubt, that she was who she was meant to be. And she felt whole, knowing that she was more than just a wife. She felt full of purpose, life, and love knowing that the man she loved, loved her, cherished her, and believed in her and her dreams.

She sighed. "There's only one thing left to do now." She slowly pulled her body away from his and rose to standing. After she had turned her back to him, she tilted her head back and whispered, "Could you...?" as she motioned to her buttons.

In a trice, he was on his feet and was undoing the excessive amount of buttons and loops and ribbons tying her dress together.

As the layers slipped down until she was left only in her nightgown, she dropped her voice low, "As I was saying..." she pulled the nightgown overhead and leaned in to brush her lips against his. "There's one thing we must do first, as husband and wife." She pressed her lips onto his, and her palms on his chest, then gave a small push. Hard enough to make him stumble back a step. "First to the other side of the pond wins!" She yelped as he tried to reach for her.

Jonathan took half a second to comprehend her meaning but was already whipping off his cravat and yanking off his boots, when he yelled back, "Wins what?" He tore off his jacket and waistcoat, but got only as far as his breeches by the time she was in the water.

"Exactly!" She laughed, not answering his question.

He tore into the water after her, intent on finishing what they had started.

Read On

R ead on for a preview of the third tale in The Good Dukes Series from Eliana Piers: *Good Duke Gone Bad*.

GOOD DUKE
GONE *Bad*

THE GOOD DUKES SERIES

ELIANA PIERS

Chapter 1

1815, England

Bella shook her head. How she had found herself in such a predicament, she was unsure, but she was relieved for herself, and her cousin, that she had been the first one to stumble upon the tryst.

Catching her cousin and her lover in the act of...whatever it was exactly that they were doing–she tried not to look too closely–had been an intervention of fate. If anyone else had caught them, it would be the scandal of the year. A duke found in the gardens alone with his best friend's younger sister.

This manhunt–womanhunt–through the garden was a terrible idea. Who had suggested it anyway? Bella recalled that it had been proposed by Lady Katherine, Kat, as everyone called her. For some reason, Kat had wanted to find out where Margaret was, mayhap her proposal was due to her own wildly impulsive nature and proclivity for impropriety. Or possibly she just loved to have something to gossip about.

There was also the slight chance of jealousy. Wasn't that often the magnet pushing and pulling women together? And wasn't that what she worked so hard to beat by accepting women for who they were and rooting for their success in life? Sometimes more than her own.

She had agreed to go on the inane hunt for two reasons: one, she wanted to befriend Kat, if only to keep possible enemies close, and two, she loved a stroll through the garden. Many flowers only released their aroma in the evening, and that was enough of a temptation for her to accept.

Her free spirit could get her into trouble ambling through the garden at night by herself, so to be fortressed by a group of people, albeit some drunk, was an excellent excuse for a midnight wander. Especially with winter around the corner, when there would be fewer opportunities. She had to get her fill of flowers whenever she could now. And then when the snow came, she would spend her time in the orangery. She was thankful that she was visiting her cousin who happened to have one of the largest orangeries around. If only her cousin had chosen the orangery as the location for her tryst, perhaps this burden wouldn't be on Bella's shoulders.

She shook her head again.

"So, who are you going to tell?" A deep voice attached to even deeper colored locks probed. He spoke quietly, so as not to raise attention from the rest of the group ahead of them. They were all heading back into Chatsworth House after the failed attempt to find Margaret. Failed, that is, according to everyone but Bella.

"To what are you referring?" Bella raised her chin in reply.

The voice rumbled out a short laugh. "So that's how it is then, is it?"

"That's exactly how it is."

"Well, as someone who makes a living reading other people and knowing their business, I'll have to call you on that."

"Why you arrogant—"

"Tut, tut, tut. Such strong words from such a slight frame. I don't know that you have what it takes to back up whatever insult, and perhaps threat, you were about to make."

Scoffing, she announced, "I'll have you know that I have connections to a duke, maybe two, who will not hesitate to come to my defense."

"But not an exclusive shield, such as a husband, to protect you. How can you be so sure they would be readily available when you needed them?"

"I am neither in want nor need a husband." *Lie.* She rushed through her falsehood and continued, "I don't envy the women who have a duke for that job." *Truth.*

He raised a brow in a perfect arch.

Equipped with only a moonlight sky and her dubious abilities to read people, even she could interpret his skepticism. She wasn't sure, however, if he was skeptical of the former or latter claim. She chose to follow up on the latter with a single shoulder shrug, "Too much hassle." Of course she wouldn't go into more detail with this egotistical acquaintance.

Out of her periphery, she caught Lyle nod.

"Quite."

One word? That was his response. With all his previous assertions that he knew everything, he was going to reply with that ambiguous response?

As Bella harrumphed and quickened her pace to catch up with the rest of the group, she heard that low, extremely irritating laugh again.

If nothing else, his one word reaffirmed to Bella her second dictum. The first, she had known without doubt for quite a while: never marry a duke. The second, unequivocally accepted and adhered to by anyone with free will, never marry an arrogant prick.

Stay Connected

Read the Rest:

Book 3 is coming soon!

Please leave me a review :)

If you like my books, please leave me a review. You can find my books through my Amazon Author page here.

https://amazon.com/author/elianapiers

Read Book 1:

Read Book 1 of the Series here: Good Duke Gone Cold here
https://www.amazon.com/dp/B0C6GG3NTJ

Read a FREE Short story:

Get my **FREE** Short Story when you sign up to join my mailing list. Plus you'll learn more about me, get sneak peeks at what's in the works, as well as access to some discounted or free books from other authors.

Sweeten the Rogue: One wager, one evening of passion, two possible futures for a rogue and a lady https://bit.ly/SweetenTheRogue

ARC Team:

If you love my books, you can sign up to join my ARC team to receive FREE advanced copies.

https://bit.ly/ElianaPiersARCSignUp

Find me and follow me online:

www.facebook.com/elianapiers

Instagram: @ElianaPiersAuthor

BONUS:

You also get a Free Regency Romance Coloring Book if you sign up for my newsletter by clicking here:

https://bit.ly/regencyromancecoloringbook

Thank You

Thank you to my fellow author and critique partner, Ally Hudson. *Honey pot. Honey pot. Honey pot.*

Thank you to my beta readers, including Jenni Simonis and Jordan Lynch. Your feedback and encouragement was incredibly motivating!

Thank you to all my ARCs (too many to list!) But special thanks to Sharon...is it seaweed? We don't know!

Thank you to my husband who nods his head and says yes while I struggle through plot issues.

Thank you to you, my *beau monde*! It means everything to have you enjoy my books.

About the Author

Eliana Piers has been writing and singing stories since she was five years old. After feeling inspired by authors like Julia Quinn, Tessa Dare, and Minerva Spencer, Eliana decided to test her quill on the page.

Writing about love and how two people come to connect and share parts of their souls with each other is now an obsession.

Eliana lives in Canada where she drinks ice caps every day.

Also By

Short Stories

Sweeten the Rogue

The Good Dukes Series

Good Duke Gone Cold

Good Duke Gone Hard

Coming soon: *Good Duke Gone Bad*

Made in United States
North Haven, CT
26 December 2023

46654043R00128